HOMICIDE AT THE VICARAGE

A VICTORIAN BOOK CLUB MYSTERY

CALLIE HUTTON

Author's website: http://calliehutton.com/

Cover design by Anna Greene

Manufactured in the United States of America

First Edition April 2023

ABOUT THE BOOK

Lord William has finally gained his desire to move his family from Bath to his country estate, Wethington Manor, west of Reading, not too far from either Bath or London. Lady Amy is a happy, contented mother to their son, and has taken up her writing once again. Their family members are close by, and all is well.

Well, maybe not.

The new village vicar is charming, polite, and serves inspiring sermons. The villagers adore him, and many young women have their eye on the handsome cleric.

However, it appears someone doesn't love him...

My utmost thanks to Mary Basden, my UK friend who proofreads my books and finds a lot of "Americanisms." Any misses are mine, not hers.

PROLOGUE

March 1893
Bath, England

"Aunt, you look absolutely stunning. And dressed for a wedding I never expected to see." Lady Amy Wethington smiled at her Aunt Margaret, the woman who raised her after Amy's mother died. She was also the woman who voiced, emphatically, that she had no desire or intention to ever marry.

"Ah, Amy," Aunt Margaret said as she reached out and cupped Amy's cheek. "A lesson I learned. Don't say 'never' or 'always.'"

"Hmm. That's not promising since you intend to make your vows today to always love, honor, and cherish Lord Exeter."

Aunt Margaret winked at her.

Her aunt had chosen a lovely pale rose satin gown that accented her small waist and enviable lissome body. She wore a small matching hat, with netting that went from the hat to tie at her neckline.

Amy's gown was a deeper rose, also satin. She wore a larger

1

hat with flowers around the brim. She'd made sure her shoes matched—since that was always a problem for her. William often wondered why, since they'd hired a lady's maid for her, she was still missing parts of her attire whenever they had plans to leave the house.

She had no idea why, but she truly loved Maddie, the lady's maid she'd hired. She was the daughter of their cook, Mrs. Randolph, and if not the best of lady's maids, she was very easy to deal with and was so very eager to please.

A knock sounded at the bedroom door. "Sister, are you ready? It is time to leave for the church." Lord Franklin Winchester, brother to Lady Margaret and father to Amy, sounded impatient.

"I think he's afraid you're going to change your mind," Amy said as she walked to the door. Her father had been badgering his sister to marry for years.

"Good morning, Papa," Amy said as she leaned in for his customary kiss on her cheek. "You look quite handsome."

He waved her off and walked into the room. He stopped in front of Aunt Margaret, a softness to his face seldom seen. "You look wonderful, Margaret."

Then he stunned them both by saying, "Are you sure you want to marry Lord Exeter?"

Amy gasped. "Papa, you've been plaguing Aunt Margaret to marry for years!"

Papa cleared his throat. "Yes. I know that." He turned his attention to the bride. "But I want to be sure you are certain you will be happy."

Tears rimmed Aunt Margaret's eyes. "Oh, Franklin. You are so…you. Yes, I will be happy, and yes, I believe it is time to go."

The three left the room and made their way downstairs to the front door where several of the servants stood, admiring Lady Margaret. The housekeeper, Mrs. Brady, wiped the corner of her eye with a lace handkerchief.

Amy looked around the house she had been raised in, remembering leaving a mere year and a half ago for her own wedding to Lord Wethington. Things had worked out quite well for her. She was truly happy and the mother of an adorable little boy, Charles George Tottenham, already almost six months old.

"What will become of the house, now that Aunt Margaret will no longer be living here?" Amy asked as they settled into the carriage.

Papa adjusted his jacket, crossed his legs, and said, "For now, it will remain empty, except for the few staff members needed to maintain it in our absence. Since I plan to relocate to the country as you and your brother have, it might be some time before it is fully occupied again. But it will be convenient to have a place here should one of us wish to spend time in Bath."

"What about the house you and Michael purchased when you moved from London?"

"My, you are an inquisitive gel this morning." Papa's smile softened his words. "If you feel the need to know, we sold that a few weeks ago. Winchester House is entailed, so it will not be sold, only used on occasion."

Amy nodded and looked out the window at the early signs of spring. Aunt Margaret and Lord Exeter had announced their engagement back in July, but her sweet aunt had wanted Amy to be her attendant, so a March wedding was planned.

The extra time after Charles's birth was supposed to give Amy time to lose the weight gained with the baby. Alas, she'd only lost a little more than a stone, so the gown she commissioned from her modiste was a bit larger than all the ones hanging in her closet. She'd returned home in tears, telling William she was now officially as large as Mrs. Dunsten's cow.

He took her in his arms and told her he loved her just the way she was, and she was no competition for the woman's cow.

Then she soothed her feelings with a cup of tea and two of the lovely biscuits Cook had made earlier.

It was a short ride from the townhouse to the church. Aunt Margaret was fortunate that the weather was quite pleasant, when one realized March in England rarely produced nice conditions.

The marriage would take place at St. Swithin's, the church Amy's parents were married in, where she was baptized, and where she and William had married. Once they'd moved to Wethington Manor after the baby had been old enough to travel, they decided to have Charles baptized at St. Agatha Church, which was in the village outside the Manor.

The driver jumped down and opened the door, extending his hand to Amy who he helped out. Papa climbed out next and turned for Aunt Margaret who, amazingly enough, looked nervous. She'd never seen her aunt as anything but calm, graceful, pleasant, and in control of herself. It appeared weddings were uneasy for everyone.

William had already left earlier for the church in their carriage, dropping her off at Winchester House on his way. Although Lord Exeter had many friends, he had asked William to stand up with him since they were soon to be family.

Her husband had looked quite elegant in his formal clothes. It was times like these that she realized how very handsome her husband was. Hopefully, little Charles would take after his papa and not his chubby mama.

When they were settled at the back of the church, the pastor signaled the organist to begin playing. Amy walked ahead of Aunt Margaret and Papa, clutching her spray of roses.

Lord Exeter looked quite happy to see Aunt Margaret. They smiled at each other, and Amy was certain theirs would be a happy marriage.

Once the ceremony was over, they all returned to Winchester House for the wedding breakfast. Amy shivered when they all sat down to eat, remembering her own wedding breakfast where her cousin had been poisoned. Hopefully, all would go well, and they would not be subjected to another murder.

She greeted her brother, Michael, Earl of Davenport, and his wife, Eloise, her best friend since forever. They had also retired to one of Papa's estates close to Newbury with their twins, Lady Madeline Anne and Lady Patricia Joan, born the same day as Charles. The two of them joined her and William at their section of the lengthy table.

Cook had prepared a feast. They had a lovely, creamed rice soup, lamb cutlets in Italian sauce, beef fillets, aspic of ham and tongue, asparagus and cream, green beans, potatoes, and strawberry ice. It was all followed, of course, with slices of wedding cake. By the time the breakfast was over, Amy felt as though she'd gained back all the weight she'd lost since Charles's birth.

Conversation was lively and pleasant, no one died, and soon it was time for the guests to depart. William and Amy intended to travel to their home by train, with their driver, Benson, returning to Wethington Manor with their carriage, which had been needed to transport the family from the townhouse to the church and back.

As they gathered their things to have Benson take them to the train station, Amy pulled on her gloves and spoke to her papa. "Papa, when are you coming for a visit? In all the time we've been at the Manor, you've only been there for Charles's baptism. We are due a visit."

Lord Winchester sighed. "You are right, Daughter. With all my grandchildren close to each other, it would be easy to see them all at once. I must admit that I've been neglectful."

"You have, Father," Michael added. "I am able to conduct our business from my home in Newbury. If you moved your household to your estate south of Guildford, you would be closer to me for business purposes and you could see the children."

Amy never thought she would see the day she encouraged Papa to visit. They had clashed over things many times in the past, but since Amy and her brother Michael had married and then produced grandchildren, Papa seemed to have mellowed a bit and was quite pleasant to be around.

"I will finish up some business in Bath, and then I will make a visit." He leaned over and gave Amy a kiss on the cheek. Then, to her surprise, pulled her in for a hug.

It had been a beautiful wedding and a delightful day.

Six months later
September 1893

"I am pregnant!" Aunt Margaret stomped into the drawing room at Wethington Manor just as Amy was playing a hand clapping game with Charles.

"What? Did you just say you are pregnant?" Amy stared at her aunt as if she had ten heads. It was well known among family members that not only did she always profess to never marry—which she did—but the thought of bearing and raising children brought shivers to her. "Aunt, I think you need to sit down. I'll order tea."

Aunt Margaret collapsed into the chair and threw her head against the back. Amy put Charles on the floor to wander around and then walked to the bell pull and requested tea when the young maid appeared. As she returned to the settee across from Aunt Margaret, it was then that she noticed her aunt, who was always well put together, looked anything but.

Her hair was a mess, her gown wrinkled, and she fiddled with a handkerchief in her lap.

"Well," Amy said as she picked up Charles and put him on her lap. "I'm assuming this is not good news?"

Aunt Margaret merely glared at her.

"Why are you here? Just to deliver the news? Your home is quite a distance from us."

Just then Aunt Margaret's husband, Lord Exeter, entered the room. "Good afternoon, Amy. I'm afraid my wife was busy sharing what she believes to be bad news and didn't have the chance to tell you, with Wethington's permission, of course, that she is to stay with you while I make a trip to Scotland."

"Of course, Margaret is welcome to stay any time and for as long as needed." William entered the room and shook hands with Exeter. "Care for a brandy?"

"That would be nice." He followed William to the sideboard and took one of the glasses of brandy William poured for them both.

Once they were settled in chairs across from the two ladies, William put his drink on the table next to him and scooped Charles from Amy's arms and settled him on his lap. The lad began to pull on William's ascot, which he ignored, until he was almost choking. Then he removed the chubby hands from his neck piece and turned the babe so he was facing away from his tempting items.

Exeter swirled the liquid in his glass. "I received a summons from my great-uncle's man in the Highlands that he is not doing well and is not expected to live beyond another week or so. We are not close, but I am his heir so I must go and straighten everything out after his death."

He took a sip of his drink. "I don't want Margaret traveling so far in her condition"—he smiled at his wife who frowned back—"and I have no idea how long it will take to tidy things up."

Amy patted Aunt Margaret's hand. "All will be well, Aunt. We will take good care of you."

Another scowl from her aunt landed on her.

"Might I offer congratulations, Exeter?" William said.

He grinned. "We are family now, let's stop this 'Exeter'. My name is Jonathan. To answer your question, I am happy to receive congratulations. I never imagined that my ripe old age of forty-seven years would see me a father." He shook his head and downed the rest of the drink. "My wife, unfortunately, sees this as a disaster."

Aunt Margaret sighed. "Not exactly a disaster, Husband. It's just something I never planned on or particularly wanted."

"But look how sweet Charles is, my dear," Jonathan said.

Just then Charles began to scream, "Mama," with his little arms out. He pitched himself backwards and slammed William in the chest with his head.

"Tea is ready, my lady." Marcus, one of the new footmen, rolled the tea cart into the room while Amy took Charles out of William's hands.

"I will bring him to the nursery and have Nanny put him down for his nap." She left the room, murmuring to a still fussing Charles.

* * *

"WHEN DO you plan to leave for Scotland?" William asked as he settled back in his chair with the baby gone. Margaret poured tea and raised her eyebrows and held up the teapot.

"Yes, I will have tea, my dear," Jonathan said.

"I as well," William added.

"I plan to leave in a day or so," Exeter said, accepting the cup of tea from his wife.

Once the tea was poured, fixed to everyone's liking, and the small sandwiches and sweets Cook had sent in were placed onto plates and passed around, William turned to Margaret. "We will be happy to have you with us. Amy and I have started a book club with some of the villagers. There is also a sewing club, and some of the church ladies meet to collect clothing and food for the less fortunate. I am certain you will find your place while you are here."

"Indeed? I'm not surprised at the book club since she's an author and belonged to one in Bath, but a sewing club?"

"She has given it her best effort, but she enjoys the book club and the efforts to provide for the poor much more."

"I take it all is quiet here at Wethington Manor and Wethingford?" Margaret spilled a couple of drops of tea on her dress and swiped it with her fingers. William was astounded since his aunt by marriage never would have merely brushed off tea.

But as he studied her, he realized she did not look like the Margaret he'd known all these years. Frankly, she could only be described as 'untidy'. He cleared his throat, realizing she had asked him a question. "Yes, things are quiet. Amy is still working on a book; Charles is eating well and seems healthy."

"See, my love, having a child about will not devastate your life," Jonathan said.

Amy entered the room. "Well, Charles settled down quite nicely and is now sound asleep."

"Tea, Amy?" Margaret asked.

"Yes. Please." She walked to where the tea cart sat and placed a few articles on her plate. "I am trying to lose the rest of the weight I gained when I carried Charles." She licked her fingers and sat. "But it doesn't seem to be working." She took a bite of a raspberry tart.

William was happy that no one commented on her statement. He'd been listening to his dear wife lamenting since Charles was born, and the lad was almost a year old. But it troubled him not that she had kept a few pounds. She was still a very pretty young woman.

"Do you have any idea of the extent of your great-uncle's holdings?" William asked.

"To some degree, perhaps, but I am afraid I will be walking into a mess since the man has been ill for some time. I just wish they had summoned me before now so I could have started on what needs to be done." He placed his teacup on the table. "I prefer not to be away when the babe is born."

"Do you know when you can expect to join me in motherhood?" Amy asked Margaret as she eyed the rest of the tarts and then firmly set her plate on the table in front of her.

"The midwife I consulted before we left gave me a tentative date of the middle of March." She shook her head. "The month of our one-year anniversary. I never would have thought..."

Amy nodded. "You have plenty of time." She turned to Jonathan. "I hope you can be back in time for Aunt Margaret's lying in, but if not, you can rest easy knowing that we will take good care of her."

Jonathan leaned forward; his forearms braced on his thighs. "Are you aware of a midwife or doctor that you can recommend? I plan to leave in a couple of days and would like to speak with whoever will be taking care of Margaret."

Margaret huffed and bit into a raspberry tart. Crumbs landed in her lap. She ignored them.

"I can certainly ask the villagers. Each time I visit the shops in Wethingford I am struck by the number of young children, all looking happy and healthy, so there must be someone who is doing a good job." She looked over at Margaret. "We can take a ride into the village tomorrow and make some inquiries."

Marcus entered the room and looked over at Exeter. "My lord, a carriage has arrived with your trunks."

"Thank you," Jonathan said. He looked over at William. "Where shall they bring our belongings?"

Amy tapped her mouth. "I believe the blue room at the end of the corridor on the first floor is ready for guests." She turned her attention to Marcus. "Instruct the driver to bring the luggage to that room. You might have to find another footman to assist."

Margaret covered her mouth, attempting to hide her yawn.

"Aunt, I believe you should take a lie down. It may take some time to get your things into the room. I can send Josephine, one of our maids, to assist you. I will summon her and have her bring you to another guest room. I will then have her unpack for you."

"Thank you, Amy. I am a tad worn out. I don't know why. The most strenuous thing I've done all day is eat two of those lovely tarts."

William and Jonathan stood as the ladies left the room.

* * *

THE NEXT AFTERNOON, Amy and Aunt Margaret left the Manor for a trip into Wethingford. The village was a good size with many shops surrounding the village green.

As with all the large estates, no longer were there the number of tenants who farmed the land and paid rent to the main house to support the nobility. While many of the men left the farms for the city to work in factories, Wethingford still had enough families who had remained and farmed the land, paying rent and providing food for the village as well as Wethington Manor.

William had explained to her when they first arrived months before that he and his ancestors had always maintained a good relationship with their tenants and those families who had remained as farmers were treated fairly.

"Wethingford is much larger than I anticipated," Aunt Margaret said as they walked, arm in arm the short distance from the Manor to the village green.

"It is. I must admit I was quite pleased. After living my

entire life in Bath with all the activities and friends there, I was concerned that I would hate it. The concern was especially daunting because both William and I prefer to raise our son in the country."

"But you seem to have adjusted quite nicely."

"Yes. I feel comfortable." She looked over at her aunt. "Are you truly upset about the baby?"

Aunt Margaret slowly shook her head. "Not entirely." She grinned. "Jonathan says we shall hire a nurse and a nanny and eventually a governess. He or she will not interrupt my life too much."

Amy mulled over her aunt's words. She had a nurse when Charles was first born and then replaced her with a nanny. Nevertheless, Amy and William spent a great deal of time with their son. Their nanny, Mrs. Grover, oftentimes complained she didn't have enough to do. It was at those times that the nanny hinted it was time for Amy and William to present a brother or sister to Charles.

She wasn't sure she was quite ready for that yet.

"Oh, look, there is Mr. Smythe." Amy headed the two of them toward a nice-looking man strolling along, glancing in store windows and stopping to talk to a person or two. "He is our vicar and has only been here about four months, but we all love him."

"He doesn't look like a vicar."

Amy tilted her head and studied the man. "What does a vicar look like?"

"Certainly not as young and handsome as that one," Aunt Margaret said with a laugh.

Amy waved as they approached him. "Good afternoon, Mr. Smythe."

"Lady Wethington, as always it is a pleasure to see you." He smiled in her direction then glanced at Aunt Margaret.

"May I present to you our vicar, Mr. Smythe. Lady Exeter is

my aunt. She raised me after my mother passed away when I was about ten years old."

"How very nice to meet you, Lady Exeter. Are you here for a visit?"

"Yes and no. Of course, I love spending time with Lady Wethington, but it appears I will be here for a while. My husband must make a trip to Scotland to handle an estate he will shortly inherit, so I am spending the time with my favorite niece."

"Aunt, I am your only niece."

Aunt Margaret laughed and patted her hand. "I know that, dear."

"May I assume you will be joining us for Sunday Service?" Mr. Smythe asked.

"Oh, yes. I rarely miss a Sunday at church."

They chatted for a bit more and then moved along.

"He is a very nice man," Aunt Margaret said as they made their way to the dressmaker's shop. "Perhaps while I am here, I will obtain dresses that will fit in a few months. Something that would work for now, and they can be let out and not lose the basic style."

"That is an excellent idea, Aunt. Mrs. Allen is a fine seamstress. She has made me several dresses since I arrived, and I was pleased with them all. You will find she has a good eye for style that works best for each of her customers."

They stopped in front of the store where several items of clothing were displayed.

"I don't feel quite up to it now. The thought of removing clothing and being pinched and prodded doesn't appeal."

"We shall return another day then."

While shopping, they inquired in a few of the shops about a midwife for Aunt Margaret and came away with two names, both women highly recommended.

"I shall send word to them to come to the Manor. If

Jonathan intends to speak with them also, it will have to be soon," Aunt Margaret said.

A few strollers passed them by. Since Amy was well known in the village, everyone they met stopped, and she introduced them to Aunt Margaret.

"You are certainly well liked, Amy," Aunt Margaret said.

Amy shrugged. "We've been here for almost a year now, and as in all villages, everyone knows everyone else." She paused for a minute. "Is there a busy village near your estate?"

"More of a town. Not as rustic as this one. I find I like the feel here."

Amy steered them toward the Duck and Hog Inn, which sat at the far end of the village green. It was a very old building, owned by the fifth generation of the McGuiness family.

"I thought we might stop for a bite to eat. We still haven't made it to the bookstore, and I do want to stop there."

Aunt Margaret smiled. "Of course, you do."

They opened the door and entered the building. It was dim after the sunshine outside.

"Amy!"

She looked over at a woman who hopped up from a table in the corner and waved frantically.

"Lady Lily! I didn't know you were coming for a visit." Amy wended her way through the tables toward her mother-in-law who sat with her husband, Mr. Colbert.

She and Aunt Margaret took seats at their table. "When did you arrive?"

"Apparently right after you two left. William told me where you were, and Edward and I decided to take a stroll. I just love this little village." She reached over and patted Amy's hand. "And the best news is we can stay as long as we want."

"How nice."

Lady Lily grinned. "Yes. Edward has retired."

2

The next evening being Wednesday, the day the village book club met at the bookstore, Amy, Mr. Colbert—she was having a hard time thinking of him as Edward—and Lady Lily climbed into the carriage, then headed to Annabelle's Attic.

Amy had explained to them that the owner of the bookstore, Mrs. Annabelle Barnes, had found a bounteous number of books in the attic of her grandmother's home when she had inherited it. She'd always loved books, so she decided to open a bookstore and started with the books she'd inherited.

"It is rather nice to see how another book club works," Mr. Colbert said as the carriage rolled forward.

"This one is like ours. Except we don't have one person who starts the conversation." Amy smiled at him since he had run their book club for years and seemed to thoroughly enjoy it. "No one seems to want to take that role. Each week we must coerce someone into doing so."

Lady Lily nudged her husband. "You could do that, dear. You did it for years."

Mr. Colbert patted his wife's hand. "One does not arrive as a possible new member of a club and begin to take over."

"Don't discount that," Amy said. "I think everyone would give a sigh of relief if you did accept that role. As much as our members love books, none of them like a leadership position."

"Why isn't William joining us?" Lady Lily asked. "He was very much a part of the other book club."

Amy grabbed the strap alongside her as the carriage hit a gouge in the road. "He does belong, but Charles had a stuffy nose today, and William decided to skip this meeting and make sure the baby is all right." Her husband was such a worrier.

Mrs. Colbert laughed. "One of the most rewarding things about being a grandmother is watching your children as parents. Very satisfying."

"That's because you did such a fine job of raising your own children, dear. From the stories I've heard from William, not all parents are as involved as you were." Mr. Colbert again patted her hand.

Lady Lily nodded. "That is true. Especially in my class. Children are shoved off onto employees to raise. Some people I have known most of my life saw very little of their children while they were growing and now commiserate with each other that they never see their grandchildren."

Amy thought back to her conversation with Aunt Margaret. According to her, she and Lord Exeter had plans to hire a nurse, a nanny, and a governess. As much as Aunt Margaret claimed to be unhappy about the coming babe, Amy was certain, given her aunt's warm and loving nature, she would not do it when the time came.

"This is a lovely bookstore, Amy," Lady Lily declared as she looked out the window when the carriage stopped in front of the shop. "It looks so very homey and comfortable."

"And Mrs. Barnes makes you feel warm and comfortable. I

especially like the fact that she not only stocks my books but gives them a prominent position in the store."

Lady Lily smiled at her as she gathered her things. "You are Lady Wethington after all, and your books certainly deserve a prominent place, my dear. You are an excellent author. I am proud to call you my daughter by marriage."

Amy felt her face grow red. Not that she wasn't used to compliments about her work, but such a glowing one from William's mother was gratifying.

As they stepped out of the carriage, Mr. Colbert said, "I agree with my wife, Amy. You are an excellent author."

Now she really felt like her face would ignite. With all three of them smiling, they entered the store.

"Well, it appears we have guests this evening," Mrs. Barnes said as they passed through the doorway to the room in the back of the store where the meeting was held.

Amy approached the owner. "Yes, Mrs. Barnes. May I introduce you to my mother-in-law, Lady Lily Colbert, and her husband, Mr. Edward Colbert."

"It is truly a pleasure to meet you both," Mrs. Barnes said. "Are you visiting Lord and Lady Wethington?"

Lady Lily removed her gloves and stuffed them into her reticule. "This might be more than a visit. Mr. Colbert has retired, and we have all the time in the world now to visit with my children and grandchild."

Mrs. Barnes took a quick glance at Amy, most likely wondering how she felt about this news, but Amy smiled. She really did love Lady Lily and Mr. Colbert. Of course, with Aunt Margaret moving in for a while, thank goodness the Manor was quite large and with thirty bedchambers, they certainly had enough room for everyone.

The group for this book club was, surprisingly, almost as well attended as her book club in Bath. Amy introduced her parents-by-marriage, and everyone warmly welcomed them.

Mr. Smythe arrived in the room and went directly to her, taking her hand in his. "Lady Wethington, what a pleasure to see you again." He looked at Lady Lily. "And who is this lovely woman?"

"Lady Lily, may I make known to you, Mr. Smythe, Vicar of the Church of St. Agatha." She returned her attention to the vicar. "Mr. Smythe, this is Lady Lily Colbert and her husband Mr. Edward Colbert. Lady Lily is Lord Wethington's mother."

Mr. Smythe offered a short bow to Lady Lily and then shook hands with Mr. Colbert. Giving Amy a quick glance, he said, "Lady Wethington, it appears you have a full house."

"Yes. But we love having our family visit," Amy said.

Mr. Smythe took a seat in between two young misses who waved frantically at him when he moved away from Amy and her parents-in-law.

Amy studied him for a bit as he interacted with the women. The man was handsome, charming, and unmarried. He was popular with his congregation and very much so with the young ladies in the village. Casseroles, cakes, biscuits, tarts, and other items arrived at his doorstep on a regular basis. Some even delivered hand-knit socks and scarves. However, he hadn't shown interest in any one particular woman but seemed to relish all their attention.

Mrs. Barnes called the meeting to order. "Who shall direct our meeting tonight?"

When no one responded, Amy raised her hand. "Mrs. Barnes, I know Mr. Colbert is new to our group, but he conducted the meetings in the book club we all belonged to in Bath. The book we're discussing tonight is one Mr. Colbert told me he has read."

The bookstore owner looked anxiously at Mr. Colbert. "Would you mind leading our group, Mr. Colbert?"

He stood and straightened his jacket. "I would be honored, Mrs. Barnes." He moved to the front of the room and quickly started a lively discussion on the very popular and recently published book, *Treasure Island* by Robert Louis Stevenson.

* * *

TWO DAYS LATER, with Lord Jonathan preparing to leave for Scotland in the morning, Amy, William, and the Colberts gathered in the drawing room, awaiting dinner.

"Amy, Persephone keeps eyeing Othello with a scary look on her face. I'm afraid she's going to eat him," Aunt Margaret said as she arrived in the room looking—well, just not like Aunt Margaret.

Amy had noticed a change in her aunt since she had arrived, but given her condition, it was normal for her to look tired and sluggish. Amy just couldn't reconcile this unkempt Aunt Margaret with the one who raised her. Aunt's hair, always without even one strand out of place, looked as though she'd left her bed after a short nap and didn't look in the mirror.

She and her husband had been at the Manor for several days now, and Aunt did not seem happy that he was to leave on the morrow. Amy was certain she'd heard Aunt Margaret crying the night before and asking her husband if he must take the trip. A clingy Aunt Margaret was also something she'd never seen before.

She cut off her musing to process her aunt's statement again in her mind. "Persephone and Othello lived in the same house for years. Why would my dog decide now to eat your bird?"

Othello was Aunt Margaret's thirty-five-year-old cockatoo who quoted Shakespeare.

She sniffed. "Because they haven't been together for a while."

William patted Aunt Margaret on her shoulder. "Do not

21

trouble yourself. Persephone will not eat Othello. If you have concerns, keep Othello in his cage."

"Why should I keep him in his cage all the time because your dog wants to eat him?"

Amy couldn't believe the conversation they were having. William, being the gracious host, merely said, "Can I get you something to drink, Margaret? Perhaps a small sherry?"

Jonathan entered the room at that moment and walked straight to his wife. "Are you well, my dear? You look a bit weary."

"I'm fine. It will take me a few moments to completely wake up from my nap." She turned to William. "Yes, I believe I will have a small sherry before dinner."

The Colberts entered next, arm-in-arm. "Did someone mention sherry?" Lady Lily said.

William poured one for his mother as well as Aunt Margaret. It didn't take long for dinner to be announced, and they all made their way into the dining room.

Even with Aunt Margaret being a tad out of sorts, it was nice to have so much company for dinner. She and William had enjoyed just the two of them dining for almost a year, but she'd forgotten how much she loved having company. She really should entertain more.

Jonathan took a sip of his wine and looked around the table. "When I was in the village earlier as Margaret napped, there was quite the brouhaha in front of the forge this afternoon."

William wiped his mouth with his napkin. "Indeed?"

He nodded. "It seems a man named Mr. Reynolds, Alex Reynolds I believe they said, confronted the vicar and threatened him."

Amy sucked in a breath. "Threatened the vicar? How awful."

Jonathan nodded. "It was quite disturbing."

"What was the problem?" William asked.

Having everyone's attention now with them all knowing

the vicar and considering him a wonderful man, he continued. "Since I am obviously new to the area, one of the observers explained to me that Reynolds has a daughter who wanted to marry one of the local lads, Joseph Hamilton, who works a farm with his father."

William nodded. "Yes, I know the family well. Very hard workers. I can't imagine why Reynolds had objected."

"Apparently the vicar married them despite Reynolds' objection. But the woman was beyond the age of consent, so it hadn't been necessary to involve Reynolds at the time."

"Oh, dear, this doesn't sound well," Lady Lily said as she covered her mouth.

"It didn't turn into fisticuffs, but Reynolds did threaten the vicar. It seems that he had a man for his daughter to marry who she had refused. Someone in the crowd mentioned that Reynolds was to get money for allowing his daughter to marry his man."

"Selling his daughter in marriage! That's terrible," Lady Margaret said.

Amy didn't comment but considered all the marriages over the years in the Upper Crust that involved a settlement between the parties for money or land to seal the nuptials. In fact, at present, there were many destitute lords marrying heiresses from America. A title for the young woman, money for the penniless lord.

She had also suspected when her father had tried to push Lord St. Vincent at her a few years ago, it was to St. Vincent's benefit, since it came out after his murder that he was in deep debt.

"How did it end?" William asked.

"Just as I arrived, two men pulled Reynolds back and dragged him off. The vicar looked shaken, but no harm was done."

"The poor man. I'm sure he was shaken. Alex Reynolds is a

large man and known to have a temper, especially when he's had too much to drink," Amy said. She didn't add that she'd heard stories of him mistreating his daughter as well as his wife when she was alive. The girl was much better off with her new husband and his family. They were lovely people.

* * *

AT CHURCH THE NEXT MORNING, after a tearful goodbye between Aunt Margaret and Jonathan, the family made their way up the steps of the lovely old building. England was full of these old churches, most of which had been built during the Tudor period, and Amy loved them.

As expected, the vicar delivered a moving homily. While she had enjoyed the sermons from the pastor at St. Swithin's, Mr. Smythe certainly moved her each week, making the prior week with its troubles appear insignificant.

"Do you wish to meet the others for the luncheon?" William took her by the elbow as they exited the church.

"Yes. I always enjoy that, but it depends on whether our guests wish to as well."

"We shall ask them." They wandered off in the direction of Aunt Margaret and his parents who were conversing with the vicar.

"Oh, you must join us," Mr. Smythe said as they walked up to the group. He nodded to William and Amy. "I was just explaining to your guests that they must come with us for the luncheon." He turned to Aunt Margaret and the Colberts. "It's a wonderful time for the congregation to be together and share a meal. Sometimes we get so involved in our daily lives we forget that human contact is so important."

"Then, in that case, we will definitely join you and all the congregants," Mr. Colbert said.

Just then Mr. Reynolds barreled his way into their group,

pointing his finger in Mr. Smythe's face. "I'm not finished with you, Vicar."

William stepped up and took Reynolds' arm. "This is not the place nor the time to discuss whatever issues you have with the vicar."

Reynolds tugged his arm away. "This is none of your business, Wethington. I had a marriage all arranged for my daughter and this man," he stepped closer to the vicar, "purposely ruined my plans."

William moved between the two men, forcing Reynolds to shift back. "It is done, Reynolds. Let it go. Your daughter has a fine husband, and as her father, you should be happy for her."

Reynolds stomped off, and the group took a deep collective breath. "You should be careful, Mr. Smythe," William said. "But now I believe we should forget this unpleasantness and move to the Fellowship Hall and enjoy a nice, peaceful meal with our neighbors."

"Very true, my lord." Mr. Smythe turned and led the rest of the congregants to the Fellowship Hall.

"Well done, Husband," Amy said as they followed the group of people walking ahead of them.

"Perhaps, but I'm a little concerned about Reynolds. He is extremely upset, and that's not good. Especially since we believe it has to do with money. That will make people do strange things."

With those words, they entered the Hall and took their seats, trying to put the unpleasantness behind them.

3

*E*loise was visiting for the day with her twins, Lady Madeline and Lady Patricia, and their nanny, Miss Payne. With the addition of Amy, Charles, and his nanny, Mrs. Grover, they made quite a group as they headed from the Manor for a stroll in the village.

It was a beautiful—albeit rare—bright sunny day. There would not be too many more days like this with September coming to a close and winter approaching.

"Can you imagine when these little ones are just starting to walk, and we all trek into the village?" Amy asked as she pushed the pram with Charles in it. The two nannies pushed Madeline and Patricia in a twin pram. All three babies were sound asleep.

"You've heard of leading strings, of course?" Eloise asked.

"I have. But I fear I would feel as though I were leading Persephone around instead of my son."

Eloise waved her hand. "You are too softhearted, Amy." She leaned over and adjusted the blanket over Madeline. "And William skipping the book club meeting because Charles had a stuffy noise is preposterous."

"How did you know that?" Amy asked.

"Lady Margaret told me while I was waiting for you in the drawing room." Eloise paused for a moment. "How is she doing? I remember feeling quite unwell during my first three months of confinement. Your aunt, who always seemed so well dressed and elegant, doesn't look like herself."

Amy shook her head. "Aunt Margaret is truly not herself. She is finishing up her third month so I'm hoping things will go better for her." She stopped pushing the pram for a moment and looked at Eloise. "Do you know I heard her weeping the night before Lord Exeter left?"

Eloise gaped at her. "Truly? Lady Margaret was weeping because her husband was leaving?"

"Yes. If I hadn't heard it myself, I would not believe it."

They headed to the village and moved the prams onto the pavement that had been placed many years before in front of all the stores and shops. Two days a week local farmers and crofters set up carts in the middle of the green, which lent a feeling of merriment to the area.

The vendors, or pedlars as they were mostly called, sold everything from grain for brewing to butter and cheese, and chapbooks, a cheap sort of publishing. The document was printed on parchment and then folded into as many as forty pages and were saddle stitched. They generally consisted of children's literature, poetry, political and religious tracts.

There were also the items made by weavers and women who had knitted warm socks, scarves, and hats for the coming winter. There were fancy embroidery items for sale. The best part for Amy had always been the food they sold. The aroma from the various carts made her mouth water. Fresh bread, savory meat pies, biscuits, and other treats that Amy told herself she should not eat because she was still trying to fit into her gowns from before Charles was born. William said he didn't care, but she did.

Because this was Tuesday, one of the scheduled days in Wethingford, the green was already a lively place. Charles woke up from his nap and began to wave his arms and make garbling noises that really didn't sound like words, but she swore she knew what he was saying.

"I will change his nappy, my lady." Mrs. Grover took the handle of the pram, smiling at Charles' babbling. As much as Amy enjoyed being a mother, she was more than happy to pass along those jobs to Nanny.

Miss Payne also marched off to follow Mrs. Grover.

"Where shall we go first?" Eloise asked.

"I love Mrs. Watkins' tea cakes. I suggest we start with her." Amy linked Eloise's arm, and they made their way through the gathering crowds.

The tea cakes were wonderful as always. They ate them out of a paper cone as they traversed the area and looked at the sweetest baby items. After much debate, Amy picked up a soft white sweater.

"These are lovely," she said to the woman behind the cart as she sat, her knitting needles moving at a speed Amy found hard to follow.

"Aye, my lady. I made them myself." She put her needles in her lap and waved at the cart full of items. "I made them all." She smiled, brown teeth, with several missing, flashed in the sun.

"It appears the lovely weather has brought out all the beautiful ladies."

Amy and Eloise turned.

"Good afternoon, Mr. Smythe. I see you are enjoying the fine air, yourself," Amy said. She smiled at Eloise. "May I present to you Mr. Smythe, our vicar. And this is Lady Eloise Davenport, my sister by marriage."

"What a pleasure to meet you, my lady. Yes, indeed, I find the weather delightful. I was writing my sermon and decided the Lord would be pleased if I took a stroll around the village and filled my eyes with his beauty." He winked at them and moved on.

Eloise studied Mr. Smythe as he strolled off. "He is your church's vicar?"

"Yes," Amy said, as she watched him stop two young ladies who turned and gazed at him with open adoration. He leaned in close, so the girls had to do the same thing. He then placed his hand at the one girl's lower back.

"He seems somewhat friendly with the ladies," Eloise said as she took Amy's arm, and they continued to stroll along.

"Yes, he does, doesn't he?" Now that it had been pointed out to her, she realized most of the times she'd seen Mr. Smythe, he was charming the women. He was a nice, handsome man, but one would think he'd be careful about touching women and encouraging his adoring admirers.

After about an hour of wandering around, Mrs. Grover and Miss Payne caught up to them. The babies were awake but content to just enjoy the ride and play with their fingers.

"That tea cake was nice, but I think I could use an actual meal," Eloise said.

"I agree. William has cautioned me about eating food from the vendors, so I think we should all traverse to the Duck and Hog Inn and enjoy a proper lunch."

"My lady, I believe we should bring the babies back to the Manor," Mrs. Grover said.

Amy tapped her lips in thought. "You are probably right. I don't like the air in the Inn. My lungs can take the smoke, but the babies' lungs cannot."

The two nannies turned the prams toward the Manor, and Eloise and Amy continued to the Inn. As expected, the smoke from the kitchen as well as those smoking cigars was not pleasant, but the food at the Duck and Hog was worth putting up with a lungful of smoke.

"I was just here with Aunt Margaret last week. We walked the village and then had lunch. William is going to ask me soon why we are paying for a cook." They both laughed as Lucy, the innkeeper's daughter who worked in the inn arrived at their table.

Once she walked away, Eloise leaned forward and lowered her voice. "It appears your vicar is not going to get his sermon finished any time soon." She nodded in the direction of a table against the wall.

Mr. Smythe sat at the table with a young woman. She was patting her eyes and wringing a handkerchief. They leaned in close to each other, and he seemed to be trying to calm her down.

Not wishing to stare at the couple, Amy looked back at Eloise.

"Who is the young lady?" Eloise asked.

Amy shrugged. "I don't know. Of course, I am not familiar with everyone in the village, but if the young lady is a church member, I don't see how I would have missed her."

"She's very pretty," Eloise said.

Lucy arrived with their food which smelled wonderful. They forgot all about the vicar and the young lady as they enjoyed their lunch.

"I miss not having you at the book club," Amy said as she reached for her glass of ale.

"I miss not going, as well. It's not a terribly long drive from Newbury Park to the Manor. Perhaps I can convince Michael to bring me here on Tuesdays. Is that the day of your meeting?"

"No, we meet on Wednesdays. It would be perfect if you and Michael stayed the night and returned home Thursday mornings."

Eloise hmmed. "I'm not sure if he would like to make that trip every week, but I will certainly ask him."

"You could bring the twins and Miss Payne, and he would never know the difference."

"Doesn't William attend the meetings? That would leave Michael alone."

Amy laughed. "And you think that would disturb him? I know my brother. He would be more than happy to drink a brandy or two and comb William's library in peace."

Eloise huffed. "Are you saying my husband would prefer silence to my company?"

Amy didn't answer but merely smiled and picked up her glass of ale.

"I'm sure William would prefer silence to your company."

Even though she didn't believe that, she didn't want to upset her friend further. "Yes. I am sure."

By the time they finished their lunch and were ready to depart, Vicar Smythe and his female companion were still speaking in low tones.

"I wonder what that is all about," Eloise asked as they stood from the table.

"It is truly none of our business. She might be looking for counselling. That is part of his job, you know."

"Yes. I hadn't thought of that." Despite her words, Eloise frowned at the two of them.

* * *

IT WAS a lively dinner with Michael, Eloise, Aunt Margaret, Lady Lily, and Mr. Colbert joining them.

"It appeared your vicar had his hands full today when Amy and I had luncheon at the Inn," Eloise said as she broke a piece of bread in half.

William looked at her with surprise. "Don't tell me Mr. Reynolds accosted him again?"

Eloise shook her head. "No. It was some young lady who was crying all over him."

"That is untrue," Amy said. Looking at the others at the table, she continued, "The woman was indeed crying, but it appeared Mr. Smythe had the situation under control."

"Who was it?" William asked.

Amy shrugged. "I don't know; I hadn't seen her before. Of course, since I don't know everyone in the village, it is no surprise that I didn't recognize her."

William returned to his dinner. "It appears the vicar has had his hands full of troubles lately."

Michael placed his wine glass on the table. "What else has happened? You mentioned a Mr. Reynolds?"

"Yes. Apparently, Reynolds has a daughter who he planned to marry off to someone who was going to give him money for the girl."

Michael shook his head. "Not good."

Once again, Amy thought of all the ton marriages that started off that way but saw no reason to comment.

William continued. "She and one of the young farmers wanted to marry. They sought the services of Mr. Smythe, and he married them since the girl was old enough to not need her father's consent."

"Money will turn some people ugly. Or I should say the opportunity to get some and be thwarted will," Michael said. "Did you see this altercation?"

"No." William shook his head. "Lord Exeter saw it when he was visiting."

"When will he return?" Eloise asked.

"We don't know. It seems he has a lot of business to take care of in Scotland."

Lady Lily looked between William and Lady Margaret. "Will he be here in time for the birth?"

Aunt Margaret pushed her chair back, almost hitting the

footman behind her. Her eyes were filled with tears. "If you will excuse me." She practically ran from the room.

Silence prevailed for a full minute, then Lady Lily said, "I'm so sorry. It sounds as though I made a mistake."

"She misses her husband," Amy said.

Michael pushed his dinner plate away, which was immediately picked up by the footman. "I must say, I've never seen my aunt so sensitive. And I never thought to see her so attached to a man that she cries because he's not here. Whatever happened to our strong, resilient Aunt Margaret?"

"She became with child," Lady Lily said.

Two days later, Amy, Aunt Margaret, and Lady Lily sat in Amy's solar and worked on embroidery. Despite her lack of talent for items done by hand—except for writing books—and with William telling her that now she was a mother and should take some time for herself and not trouble making desserts for him anymore, she was determined to finish the lovely picture of a puppy to hang on the wall in Charles' nursery.

"Dear, I believe you missed a couple of stitches there," Lady Lily pointed out.

Amy held up the cloth. "Yes. I believe you are correct." She huffed and placed her poor attempt on her lap. "I do not find these things easy to do."

"True," Lady Lily said. "But you are an intelligent woman. I am sure you will be able to finish it."

Aunt Margaret sat with her endeavor in her lap as she gazed out the window at the gloomy day. A reminder that winter was on its way.

She sighed. "I wonder if Jonathan has arrived at his uncle's house yet." Her voice was soft and low. Her dress was wrinkled, her hair doing a good job of escaping from her topknot, and there were dark circles under her eyes.

"Are you feeling unwell, Aunt?" Amy asked.

Aunt Margaret turned to her. "Yes."

Well, then.

"Can I get something for you? Should I send for tea?"

Lady Lily looked up from her work. "My dear, we had breakfast only an hour ago."

Aunt Margaret waved at her. "No, I do not care for tea right now." She carefully wiped the tear from the corner of her eye, took a deep breath, and picked up her embroidery again. Without much enthusiasm.

Amy was truly growing concerned about Aunt Margaret. Perhaps it had not been the best decision Jonathan had made when he thought she would be better off here than travelling with him to Scotland. Aunt was well into her third month and soon would be the time when she should be feeling better and enjoying the pregnancy. Of course, Aunt Margaret had shown little enthusiasm for the coming birth of her child.

"Aunt, we have been remiss in securing the services of a midwife. With Jonathan already gone without being able to see anyone, I think I shall summon one of the women from our list."

"Yes, Jonathan apologized for not taking care of that before he left. He asked me to secure someone's services as soon as possible. I am to send word when I have been seen by someone here—either a midwife or a doctor."

"I will send a message to Mrs. Townsend who I understand is an excellent midwife and ask her to attend you."

Despite Amy's enthusiasm, Aunt Margaret merely nodded.

"My lady, you have visitors." Filbert, William's butler for years, who had traveled with them from Bath to the Manor, entered the room with his usual aplomb.

"Visitors?" She didn't usually have visitors until the afternoon. "Who is here?"

"Mrs. Applegate and Miss Martin."

Amy looked over at Lady Lily and Aunt Margaret. "Two members of the book club. I wonder what brings them here?"

"Perhaps you should have Filbert escort them up," Lady Margaret said.

"Yes. Of course." She looked up at Filbert. "Please conduct the two women to us."

Filbert left and within seconds, it seemed, the two women rushed into the room. Mrs. Applegate placed her hand on her impressive bosom, attempting to catch her breath.

"Please, Mrs. Applegate, Miss Martin, have a seat," Amy said.

Once seated, Mrs. Applegate turned to her. "Have you heard the news, my lady?"

Not having received any news that would cause her to be as disconcerted as the two women seemed to be, she said, "No. Nothing unusual."

"Mr. Smythe is dead!" Mrs. Applegate almost shouted.

"Dead?" Amy asked, fighting for breath herself. "My sister-in-law and I saw him only two days ago. He seemed in the best of health."

"There was indeed no problem with the man's health. He was shot!" Miss Martin fanned her face with her hand.

Aunt Margaret perked up and looked at Amy. "Another one, Niece? I'm thinking it was not safe for Jonathan to have left me here."

Miss Martin and Mrs. Applegate stared at Aunt Margaret, then turned their attention to Amy.

"Another one? Has someone else died?" Mrs. Applegate asked.

Amy glared at her aunt.

4

*W*illiam made the rounds of visiting his tenants and was happy to learn that no one was having a major problem, and all was well. His last stop, with Mr. and Mrs. Gabel, would take some time he knew, because Mrs. Gabel always insisted he stay for a meal or if it wasn't mealtime, then for tea.

After trekking back and forth to his tenants' homes and taking note of their fields and strong, healthy animals, he would have preferred a tall mug of ale.

"Good day, my lord," Mr. Gabel said as William dismounted from Major, his Cleveland Bay Horse.

"And as well to you, Mr. Gabel." He straightened his clothes and preceded the man into his house.

Mrs. Gabel held the door opened for him. "My lord. It is always pleasant when you visit us."

The three of them settled around the small kitchen table. The Gabels were well into their fifties. They had produced one daughter and one son. Their daughter, Minerva, married a man from Scotland and made her home with him there. Luke Gabel joined the Royal Navy and only appeared occasionally to visit with his parents.

From what William had learned after his return from Bath, father and son didn't see eye to eye on most things, so even though it made for more work for Mr. Gabel, both he and his wife were relieved when their son left.

Once Mrs. Gabel had produced her special teapot, cups, saucers, small plates, and a tray of biscuits and tarts, William leaned back in his chair and addressed his tenant. "Are there any problems I should be aware of, Mr. Gabel?"

The man took out a pipe and stuffed it with tobacco. "Nothing, my lord. All is well. It appears we will have a very good harvest this year. Young Abel Jenkins has been helping me and we are almost finished."

William took a sip of tea. "Then we must have a grand Harvest Festival this year."

"Oh, that would be wonderful, my lord," Mrs. Gabel said as she settled into her chair. "We didn't have them when you were living in Bath. I was hoping after returning with your lovely family that you would bring the Festival back. I know the ladies have been hoping to enter their jams and baked goods into the contests we always held."

William nodded. "I will have my wife set things up. Perhaps mid-October? The weather should still be mild. Do you think that will give everyone time to prepare?"

Mrs. Gabel nodded. "That should be fine. It will give us more than three weeks." She clapped her hands. "The ladies will be so excited."

"Can I count on you to spread the word? Once I check with Lady Wethington, I will be able to give you a precise date."

"Of course, my lord."

William couldn't help but compare social events to those who lived in the country and those in the cities. In Bath and London, social events involving the nobility were expensive and were mainly meant to impress. In the country, it was for fun, socializing, and competing against each other. Truth be told, he preferred the country way of life and was glad he'd moved his family here where it was peaceful and quiet and dead bodies would not be turning up.

"I would love if you would bring Lady Wethington one time when you visit. I have spoken to her a few times when we met in the village."

"I will do that, Mrs. Gabel. She's been so busy with the baby and her books, but she needs to take some time for enjoyment."

"Her books, my lord?" Mrs. Gabel asked.

William offered them a bright smile. "Yes, indeed. Did you not know my wife is an author?"

Mrs. Gabel placed her hand on her chest. "No, I did not know that. Has she published a book yet?"

"She certainly has. Do you read much?"

The woman shook her head. "I'm afraid I never have time for that, but I am impressed that we have an author right here in Wethingford." She looked over at her husband. "Who would have known that her ladyship is an author."

Mr. Gabel placed his pipe on a chipped plate that was most likely provided by his wife to be used for his pipe. "I'm afraid I don't read much either. I'm grateful that the village bookstore carries the Bath and Bristol newspapers so I can at least read what's happening in the world, even if they are a few days late when they get them."

William stood. "I have thoroughly enjoyed our visit. I'm happy all is well with you, but remember, if anything arises that you can't do yourself, just send word to the Manor, and I will have someone assist you."

"Thank you, my lord. That is quite generous."

As William strode to his horse, mounted, and headed home, he pondered on how happy Amy would be about the upcoming Harvest Festival. Planning and organizing it all might not be her strongest points, but with Lady Margaret and his parents living with them, she would have a lot of help.

A carriage was just leaving the Manor as he rode into the stable. He left his horse with one of the younger grooms and headed to the house.

"I assume her ladyship is home?" William asked as he handed his outer jacket and hat to Filbert.

"Yes, my lord. She and Lady Exeter and Lady Lily are in her solar."

"Thank you." He bolted up the stairs to the sound of female voices speaking over each other.

The women were waving their hands and appeared very excited.

"Good afternoon, ladies. What has you all in a dither?" He took the seat on the settee, next to Amy. They all quieted.

Amy took a couple of breaths and said, "Mr. Smythe is dead."

William reared back. "The Vicar?"

"Yes." She took another deep breath. "And it was murder, William. He died from a shotgun wound."

Bloody hell.

* * *

EVEN AFTER MRS. APPLEGATE and Miss Martin had all exclaimed over Mr. Smythe, shed a few tears, and then left, Amy was still in shock. Everyone loved Mr. Smythe!

Well, apparently, not everyone.

William studied her for a moment. "You don't look well, my love. I think a drop of brandy is called for." He looked at the other two women. "I think we can all use a bit of spirits."

"I would prefer tea," his mother said. "To put my brandy into," she added.

He left the room, and Amy brushed back the hair from her

forehead with a shaky hand. "I have dealt with murders before —as you all know—but I never imagined I would see it again in this lovely quiet village."

"My dear," Lady Lily said, "murder happens everywhere."

"Everywhere Amy and William live," Aunt Margaret said. "I've told you before, Niece, you and your husband are not safe people to be around."

Discounting her comments, Amy said, "I believe as Lord of Wethingford, William is responsible for arranging for the police and coroner to arrive."

When William returned to the room with a footman in tow, carrying a teapot, cups, saucers, and a brandy bottle, Amy said, "I believe we need to be involved in this, William."

He took his seat again and poured a small amount of brandy into each teacup while Amy fixed the tea for everyone.

"As much as I would like to stay out of this, you are correct. I must go visit the vicarage and ask questions of those who found him. Did the ladies who brought you the news say how the body was found?"

"No," Lady Lily said as she took a sip of her tea, then made a face. "They were so very excited to pass the news around, none of us thought to ask for any additional information."

Amy reached over and placed her hand on William's knee. "We must go to the vicarage and find out what has happened so far."

He stared at her. "Why would you have to go, my dear?"

She drew herself up. "Why wouldn't I go? It is your responsibility to get this matter taken care of, and I am your wife."

"And?"

"Oh, William, please don't pretend to all of us that you think Amy will not become involved in this. She's been through such a thing before. Many times, in fact." Aunt Margaret downed her tea and stood. "You may all decide what you want to do about this. That little bit of brandy has made me drowsy. I think I will take a short nap before dinner."

"I am with you, Margaret," Lady Lily said as she also stood and shook out her skirts. "The brandy and tea have restored my nerves, so I believe a bit of a lie-down is just the thing."

William glanced at Amy when the room emptied. "Are you not tired, darling? Shouldn't you take a bit of a rest also?"

She wagged her finger and smiled. "Oh, no, you don't. I am going with you."

"What about Charles?"

"He is much too young to be involved in murder investigations."

"Do not toy with me, Amy. I think as his mother you should stay here and take care of him."

"Mrs. Grover has things well in hand." She stood and moved toward the door. "I will just freshen up and meet you downstairs." She turned before she passed through the doorway. "Do not attempt to leave without me. I will merely follow you. I do know where the vicarage is."

Amy checked briefly on Charles and found him busily playing on the floor with his various toys. She cuddled him and spoke with him for a bit—even though he voiced gibberish baby talk, and then kissed him and handed him over to Nanny. "I expect his lordship and I will be back in time to visit with Charles before dinner, but since we have something to take care of in the village, if it gets too late, just put him to bed."

As a dutiful husband, William waited for her at the bottom of the stairs. "I had the carriage brought around in case it gets too late to return on foot." He took her hand in his and linked their fingers. "How is Charles?"

"Just fine. As happy to see me leave as he was to see me arrive." She thought for a minute. "Should that bother me?"

They settled into the carriage. "Why should that bother

you? Do you want to raise a clingy child? One who wails every time you leave the room?"

She shook her head. "No. I just don't want Mrs. Grover to take my place in his affections."

"My dear, you must stay awake nights thinking of things you should be concerned about. I had a nanny and then a governess until I left for school. Do I appear to you to hold motherly affections toward anyone except my mother?"

"No."

"How was your childhood? I can't believe Lady Margaret spent all her waking hours with you."

"No. My mother died when I was about ten years. Papa was more than happy to leave me with Aunt Margaret where I had been all my life. As you know, my aunt is a lovely person, but not what one would call the motherly type."

William looked out the window as they approached the vicarage. "It seems your aunt will have to assume some motherly feelings soon."

Several people stood outside the vicarage and looked relieved when they saw the Wethington carriage arrive. William helped Amy out and they walked up to the door.

"Who found Mr. Smythe?" William scanned the crowd.

"Herbert did, my lord," Mr. Jackson, the local stonemason said.

"Herbert Moore?" William asked.

"Yes. He had business with Mr. Smythe and knocked and knocked and no one answered, so he opened the door and found him in his library." He stopped for effect. "Dead."

"His housekeeper was not at the vicarage?" William asked as he walked toward the vicarage door.

"No. Mrs. Peters was out shopping. When she arrived, Moore was just coming out of the house, pretty upset, they said."

William turned to Amy. "I do not want you to come into the vicarage until I see what the situation is."

For once, Amy was happy to obey his wishes. If it was a gunshot, who knew what the body looked like? Certainly not something she wanted to see before dinner.

About ten minutes later, William came out of the vicarage. He looked a bit rattled, but not extremely so. She turned to Mrs. Hemphill who was standing with the rest of the crowd. "Where is Mrs. Peters?"

"Oh, my lady, when she returned about an hour ago, she heard what had happened and nearly passed out on us. Mrs. Watters took her to her house."

William spoke to a few of the men in the crowd around the vicarage, then he moved toward her. "He is dead. A gunshot wound to his chest. I'll have to notify the Magistrate in Reading to send a coroner and someone to investigate the murder."

He turned toward the crowd. "I must ask all of you to return to your homes. I will be traveling to Reading tonight to notify the Magistrate and have him send someone here to take care of things. Please, also, do not attempt to enter the vicarage. Whoever comes to investigate this will not want anything touched."

William and Amy waited until the crowd dispersed. Once they were gone, he said, "We must go to Mrs. Watters' home and speak with Mrs. Peters. The poor woman must be quite distressed."

As they walked the short distance from the vicarage to Mrs. Watters' house, Amy said, "Are you riding for the Magistrate tonight?"

William shook his head and took her elbow to keep her from tripping over a small rock. "I don't think it's necessary. I'm sure the Magistrate is settling in for the night. I will have one of our footmen go to the vicarage and stand guard to make sure no one enters. Then I can make the trip to Reading tomorrow."

"I shall go with you to Reading tomorrow." She stared at him, waiting for his refusal.

"Amy, dear, marriage to you tells me if I said no, I can be quite sure I will find you strapped to the boot of the carriage or sitting up with Benson when I attempt to leave."

She grinned. "See how much easier things are when you don't disagree with me?"

They arrived at Mrs. Watters' door and knocked. She opened, looking quite flustered. "Oh, my lord, I am so glad you are here. Mrs. Peters has been quite disconcerted, waiting for you to arrive. She's been babbling the entire time."

William turned to Amy, both with raised eyebrows. "May we come in, Mrs. Watters?"

"Oh, yes, of course, I am so sorry, my lord, my lady." She stepped back and allowed them into the room.

Mrs. Peters rose from the settee where she'd been dabbing her eyes with her handkerchief. She took a deep breath and said, "My lord, I know who killed our dear vicar."

5

*W*illiam gently approached the woman and placed his hand on her shoulder. "Please try to calm yourself, Mrs. Peters. We will get this all sorted out."

"It was him, that horrid Mr. Reynolds who threatened our dear vicar. He is known to be violent, especially when he drinks, and he was quite soused last night at the Inn, talking about how he hated Mr. Smythe and because of his actions, he lost a lot of money."

"Now, Mrs. Peters, we cannot make accusations like this without proof." He held up his hand as she began to speak. "You must trust me in this. We can only accuse someone if we actually saw it happen."

"Mr. Smythe was by far one of the nicest vicars I ever worked for," she wailed as she collapsed onto the settee.

Amy sat beside her and took her hand in hers. "I assume you were not at the vicarage when you heard about Mr. Smythe?"

Mrs. Peters shook her head, white wisps from her topknot landing on her wet cheek. "I was returning from my shopping when I was stopped at the door by Mr. Moore who was speaking with Mr. Jackson, the stonemason."

"What did they tell you?" William asked.

"That I could not go into the vicarage because a crime had been committed. I had assumed someone broke in and stole things." She looked at William. "That would be an odd occurrence here. We have no crime."

Since murder could be considered a crime, Amy chose to ignore the woman's words since she was a tad discombobulated.

"What time did you leave the vicarage?" William asked.

"I never went there today. Wednesday is the day I do my shopping for the vicarage, so I left from my house, did my shopping, stopped back at my house to pick up a few things, and then arrived there."

"I assume you do not live at the vicarage?"

The woman shook her head. "It would not be proper with me and a single man living together." She looked at him as if he'd forgotten his early Bible lessons.

"Yes, that is true." William thought for a minute. "I suggest you allow us to escort you home. You might consider taking a tisane to help you sleep. I will ride to Reading tomorrow and notify the Magistrate and send a message off to the bishop advising him of today's occurrence."

"Do you have a tisane at home, Mrs. Peters?" Amy asked.

"Yes. I do keep nerve powder on hand for difficult occasions."

Amy and Mrs. Peters stood and walked toward the door.

William stopped and turned to Mrs. Watters. "Thank you for allowing Mrs. Peters to recover here."

"It was no problem, my lord." She walked them all the way out to their carriage.

Amy settled next to Mrs. Peters in the carriage. "Where are the items you purchased for the vicarage today?"

"Oh, my goodness. I don't know what happened to them. Once they told me the horrible news, I was so distraught I couldn't think, and then Mrs. Watters brought me to her house."

Amy patted her hand again. "I'm sure we can find them. Everything will get straightened out."

"Oh, my goodness," Mrs. Peters said. "What will become of my job?"

"Mrs. Peters, I'm sure the bishop will send another vicar to replace Mr. Smythe. You must have been through changing of vicars in your time there. I will mention we need a replacement when I send the missive to him tomorrow."

"If you need anything, please let us know. We can certainly help until your job resumes," Amy said.

"Yes. I will see that your pay remains in place."

Mrs. Peters burst into tears. "You are so wonderful, my lord, and you too, my lady, but I couldn't accept charity."

Amy took a quick glance at William and said, "We can certainly use more help up at the Manor, so you can work for us until a new vicar arrives."

Again, the poor woman cried and thanked them over and over. Fortunately, the carriage rolled up to Mrs. Peters' house. Benson jumped down and helped Mrs. Peters out, then up to her door.

"Try to get some rest, and I will speak with you tomorrow," William called as they watched her hobble away, clinging to the driver's arm.

Benson returned, climbed up to the driver's seat and the carriage moved forward.

Amy blew out a deep breath. "She is quite distraught."

"Not everyone is as familiar with murder as we are, my dear."

They were silent for the remainder of the trip. Once they

entered the house, Filbert informed them dinner would be ready in about a half hour unless they wished to postpone it.

"Has Charles already been put to bed?"

"Yes, my lady. Mrs. Grover brought him down and he visited with Lady Exeter in your absence."

That was promising. Her aunt hadn't sent the boy away with orders to never subject her to entertaining him again.

"Do not have Cook postpone dinner," William said, looking to Amy for agreement. "We will merely freshen up and be back down again. I don't want to keep the others from their dinner."

Filbert bowed and headed for the kitchen.

"Truth be known, I would prefer a tray in our room, but I know everyone will be waiting to hear what happened when we arrived at the vicarage," Amy said as she wearily climbed the stairs.

"I can certainly join them for dinner, and you can have a tray sent up. You do look a tad fatigued."

Amy shook her head as they reached their bedchamber door. "No need. I'm sure the food will restore me."

"As you say," he stated as he opened the door and ushered her in.

* * *

WILLIAM TRIED his best to have Amy remain at home when she still looked tired in the morning, but she refused.

"I am perfectly fine, William. There is no reason I should not go with you." She covered her mouth as she yawned.

They were climbing into the carriage for the trip to Reading which would take about two hours if the roads were in good shape. William was up early, allowing Amy to get some more sleep, and spent the time in his study, penning a note to the bishop since he was temporarily in Newbury, the opposite direction from Reading and he felt the man should be told as soon as possible about his vicar's death.

They had a quick breakfast with Mr. Colbert since William's mother and Lady Margaret were still abed. Where he had tried to convince Amy to remain.

"What is it you have there?" Amy asked as she gestured toward the papers in his hands.

"Notes I made this morning about what happened yesterday. Who found the vicar, what the situation was, and that I've had the vicarage guarded since the murder was made known to me."

"I hope you changed guards so whoever you sent out there could get some sleep."

"My dear, have you ever known me to forget about someone doing me a service?"

"No." She smiled at him. "You are a most efficient man, Husband."

William snapped his fingers. "I just now remembered that when I visited with Mr. and Mrs. Gabel yesterday, Mrs. Gabel reminded me that the years I was in Bath, the village did not hold a Harvest Festival. I remember as a boy how much I enjoyed it, and the villagers as well. I felt bad when she said so because there had been no reason why I could not return each year and hold it for them."

"I love that idea! I was never involved in one because I lived my whole life in Bath with my mother and Aunt Margaret. Even my boarding school was not far from Bath. Some of the girls spoke of the Harvest Festival at their homes, and I was always envious."

"And now, my dear, you have a chance to not only attend one, but make all the arrangements."

Amy's eyes grew wide. "Oh, dear. Since I've never attended a Festival, I have no idea how to arrange one. I guess I will start with Mrs. Gabel. I'm sure she has several friends who would be more than happy to help."

"Yes, she mentioned how the ladies loved to compete with each other in their needlework, jams, and baked goods."

"Oh, this will be a lot of fun." Amy paused. "With the passing of Mr. Smythe, though, we won't be able to hold it anytime soon."

"I suggested to Mrs. Gabel mid-October, which gives us almost a month. I think the village will have recovered by then. It will make for a nice respite from the grief of the situation."

Amy sighed and looked out the window. "I do hate these murders always dropping in front of us." She looked back at William. "Aunt Margaret said she didn't think it was wise for Lord Exeter to leave her with us."

"Come here," he said, taking her hand and pulling her so she sat next to him. He held her hand in his, rubbing his thumb over the inside of her wrist. "Your Aunt Margaret is not herself. We've both noticed her demeanor is not as cheerful as it usually is, and even her appearance has changed. She is not the woman you've known all your life. Frankly, I don't think it was a good idea for Jonathan to leave her with the frame of mind she is in. But that wasn't my decision, and I think we should just try our best to make her comfortable and don't take too much to heart what she says."

She looked up at him. "Would you have left me if my pregnancy had changed me so much?"

"My dear, I would have run for the hills."

She elbowed him. "I was being serious."

"No. If it was something I absolutely had to do, I would bring you with me and just make the trip as easy on you as possible."

She leaned her head on his shoulder. "Thank you for that."

After a few minutes, Amy sat up and pulled out a notepad and small pencil from her reticule.

"Your book?" William asked.

"Yes. With the move to the country, the additional duties I have as lady of the manor, and tending to Charles as much as I can, I'm finding it quite hard to allow time to write. I carry this with me so I can jot down thoughts when away from my manuscript."

"I'm afraid the Harvest Festival will take even more of your time."

"Yes, but I am excited about doing it."

"What I suggest you do is set aside an hour each day after breakfast and lock yourself away in your office. Tend to nothing, and make it known among the staff that unless Charles is sick or injured, no one is to disturb you during that time. If the house is on fire, then of course they should tap on your door, but otherwise, that time is yours."

Amy returned to her seat. "I get dizzy riding backward." She adjusted her skirts and said, "That is a good idea. If I could have one solid hour of no interruptions to write, I could get a lot done. If not a lot, well, then at least enough to feel as though I am moving forward with my story."

As they approached Reading, the difference in the amount of traffic and noise had increased. Amy pushed the curtain aside and gazed out the window. "I had forgotten how busy town life is."

"Do you miss it?" William asked.

"No. Well, maybe a little since it's much easier to find things you need in the city than in our small village. But I find our once-a-month trip here or Newbury when we visit Eloise and Michael is sufficient."

The Magistrate's office was in an older building on a corner. It also housed the police and investigators, William had learned when he'd had reasons to visit years ago when he first took over his title and estate.

William didn't wait for Benson to jump down and instead

opened the door himself. He climbed out and turned to assist Amy. "I hope we find the Magistrate in. If not, we'll just have to deal with the police. At least get the crime reported and have a coroner come out and remove the body."

Amy shivered when they entered the building. It was just as old and decrepit looking on the inside as it was on the outside. They both walked up to a man dressed in the familiar constable uniform sitting behind a desk.

"Good morning, sir. I am Lord William Wethington, and this is my wife, Lady Wethington. We are here to report a crime in our village."

The man leaned back and studied them. "Is that right? And what sort of a crime are you reporting? Did someone steal your wife's pretty jewelry?" He grinned, and William felt heat rise in his body.

"Is the Magistrate in? My estate and village are under his jurisdiction. If it does not trouble you too much, may we ask you to arrange for us to see him about a murder?"

he man's demeanor immediately changed as he stood up. "Yes, my lord, I will speak with the Magistrate and arrange for him to see you."

William nodded and took Amy's elbow to move them to the hard wooden bench against the wall. It took only about five minutes before the bobby returned. "My lord, Sir Archibald Regan will see you now."

They stood and followed the bobby down a long corridor into an even older part of the building. The walls were in dire need of new paint and the flooring was almost worn down to the dirt underneath.

The bobby stood at a door and tapped on it lightly.

"Yes, you may enter. You've already told me who wanted to see me." The voice was old and abrasive.

William and Amy entered the office. The Magistrate was at least ninety years old. He had scant white hair that hung over his collar. His pale blue eyes looked past them, making William wonder if the man had vision problems.

He waved at the two chairs in front of his desk. "Sit, sit, you're giving me a crick in my neck having to look up at you."

The constable who had brought them there made a quick retreat as William and Amy sat in the chairs indicated.

"A murder, eh?" The Magistrate asked.

"Yes, sir. Our vicar was found dead from a gunshot wound yesterday."

The Magistrate stopped and blew his nose in a white hand-kerchief and stuffed it into his jacket pocket. "Is he buried yet?"

Amy and William looked at each other. "No, sir," William said. "We intend to hold a funeral once we have your permission."

Sir Archibald waved his hand. "You can bury the man."

William leaned forward. "Sir, need I reiterate that this is a murder. An investigation needs to be done. A coroner should view the body and make a report."

A coughing fit overtook the Magistrate as they sat and watched him. He reached over and picked up a bottle of whisky, took a swig, and put it back. "I'll see about getting Mr. Mackay out there." He looked at them, or as close as he could look at them since William was sure by this time he had poor vision, along with other things. Why he was not wearing spectacles was questionable.

Amy addressed the man. "Is he the coroner?"

"Who?"

William didn't know whether to laugh or growl. "Mr. Mackay."

"Closest thing we have to one," he said. "Now you must excuse me. I have important things to do."

Apparently, the magistrate did not consider murder important.

"What about an investigator or constable?" Amy said.

"Why?"

William reined in his anger and spoke slowly. "Sir Archibald, I have made numerous requests to your office to assign a constable to Wethingford, yet you ignore my appeals.

Now a man has been murdered. Someone must investigate and find the murderer."

"Rarely trouble in these little villages. We don't have enough men to wander around and talk to people. If the man is dead, most likely he deserved it."

Amy gritted her teeth. "As we said, *Sir Archibald*, the man who was murdered was a vicar."

He waved a dismissal at her. "Then trouble the Church with this. They have a greater interest than we do."

Stunned at the man's attitude, William asked, "Can we assume you will send Mr. Mackay to examine the body, determine the time of death, and other necessities in a murder investigation?"

The Magistrate peered at him, his eyes narrowing. "Sounds like you know what to do yourself, Wethington." He waved them both off. "You may leave now. Send me a report."

They would obviously get nowhere with this man. William would be happy if this Mr. Mackay showed up. As they reached the door, William turned back. "When may we expect Mr. Mackay? We must get Vicar Smythe buried."

"I'll send him tomorrow. Now go. Send me a report."

They said nothing to each other for the first several minutes of the ride back home. Finally, it appeared Amy could not contain herself. "What the hell did we just witness?"

Although she never used foul language, William was so distracted by the interview they'd just had that he didn't even react to his wife's outburst.

William rubbed his forehead, attempting to dislodge the session they just experienced. "We thought Detectives Carson and Marsh were bad. At least they took notes, asked questions, *tried* to solve the murders."

"Is there no one higher up that we can go to about this? The Magistrate's behavior was ridiculous. He's telling us to solve the murder and send him a report! When were we added to the Magistrate's payroll?" Amy asked.

William slumped in the corner of the carriage. "I think we deserve a nice hearty meal before we continue our trip." He tapped on the ceiling to gain Benson's attention. "With a very large glass of ale," he added.

The small gap in the ceiling opened. "Yes, my lord. What can I do for you?"

"There is an Inn on our way back to Wethingford. It is only a mile or two from here. Please stop as her ladyship and I wish to have luncheon."

"Yes, my lord," he said and closed the opening.

"I agree, Husband. We are in dire need of a glass of ale and some food."

William was unable to hold a conversation since a combination of anger and disbelief had his thoughts running in circles. Amy seemed to be in the same state, so they remained silent until they stopped in front of The Black and Gold Lyon. They had eaten there several times after trips to Reading and were happy with the fare they would receive.

"We will be about an hour. Why don't you tend to the horses and get a meal for yourself?" William said to Benson as they made their way up the stone pathway to the old building.

The structure had been built during the reign of Henry VIII, and it was rumored that he stopped, ate, and slept in the place many times. The familiar smell of roasted meat and centuries of smoke mingled together to give the pub a sense of history and welcome.

There was only a common room, as was the same in most pubs along the road to Reading. William and Amy made themselves comfortable at a small round table near the front door. Before they even settled themselves, a serving girl brought them both large mugs of ale.

They ordered the dish of the day—rabbit stew—and took a sip of their drink.

"Now, I feel as though I can address what we just went through," William said.

"You know I couldn't put this in one of my books because it is unbelievable. I know the Lord of the Manor oversees dealing with minor incidences and feuds, but that man's treatment of a murder is unforgiveable. I do wish there was someone else we could appeal to." Amy took a rather hefty gulp of her ale.

"One thing that does surprise me is your outrage at being told to solve a murder," William said. He looked up and thanked the serving girl who placed two bowls of stew and a small loaf of bread and butter in front of them.

Amy took a slice of bread and tore it in two before buttering it. "It is strange, is it not? But I'm just put out that he assumes murder is not a major crime and informs whoever stops into his office to report such an event to deal with it themselves."

"Amy, the man must be near ninety years. I don't even know why they allow him to keep his position."

And so went the rest of their meal.

Once the carriage began its trip home, Amy took out her notepad and pencil. "We have to come up with suspects."

William smirked. "This sounds familiar."

She began to write. "Of course, we do have to include Mr. Reynolds on our list. It's Alex Reynolds, is that correct?"

"Yes." William crossed his arms. "I don't know anyone else we can add to the list. Mr. Smythe was very popular. The ladies all liked him—"

"—I just remembered when Eloise and I had lunch at the Duck and Hog on Monday, I believe it was. There was a very distraught woman at one of the tables with Mr. Smythe. I'm sure I mentioned it at dinner that night."

"Yes, I remember that. I don't see how that would make her a suspect."

"It was the day before he was killed. I think it is worth it to at least speak with her. Find out why she was so upset."

William nodded. "Write her down."

"I think we need to ruminate on this. Talk to a few people in the village. See if there are others who had a problem with the man." She paused. "William, do you think it is possible it was merely someone who broke into the vicarage to steal what he could, and Mr. Smythe surprised him and then was shot?"

"Right now, my dear, any theory would hold. It's important for the so-called coroner to give his findings on the time of death. That would certainly help with coming up with more suspects."

* * *

MAYHEM REIGNED in the nursery as Amy and William entered the room. Mrs. Peters and Mrs. Grover were shouting at each other as Charles sat on the floor crying. Amy rushed over and picked him up. He put his thumb in his mouth and laid his head on her chest.

"What is going on in here?" William asked in a not-so-pleasant voice.

Both women began to speak at the same time. He held up his hand. "One at a time, please." He nodded at Mrs. Grover. "What is the problem?"

She stiffened her back and raised her chin. "I had always assumed you and Lady Wethington were happy with the way I take care of Charles."

"Of course, we are," Amy said as she rocked her now calmed son back and forth.

Mrs. Grover pointed at Mrs. Peters. "She has arrived with instructions, she said, to assist me."

Amy could hear William groan even though the two women who stared at each other were far enough away not to hear.

"Mrs. Peters, we are very happy to have you with us for a *short time*," he emphasized as he looked at Mrs. Grover, "but we were about to tell you that Dawson, our gardener, needs help and I'm sure that is a better place for you."

She drew herself up and dipped. "Yes, my lord. I shall be happy to assist your gardener."

"Why don't you return home now, and you can assume your new duties in the morning."

She dipped again, first at William and then at Amy.

Amy looked at a still distraught Nanny. "Mrs. Grover, we had planned to spend some time with Charles. Why don't you take a nice break. Go to the kitchen and get some tea and a few of Cook's biscuits."

William watched Mrs. Grover leave the nursery. "I do hope the bishop sends a replacement for Mr. Smythe soon."

They sat on the carpeted floor with Charles, enjoying the silence after the brouhaha with the two ladies. It was a silent agreement between them that they would put the vicar's murder aside for the night and simply enjoy their son.

"Did you see that?" William asked.

"What?"

"I showed Charles his toy horse and then put it behind my back and asked him where it was, and he looked behind me."

Amy didn't have the heart to tell him she'd done the same thing with Persephone numerous times. "That is wonderful, William!"

"He is very intelligent," his proud father said. "I'm sure he will take Firsts at University."

Amy laughed. "Husband, I agree Charles is intelligent, but let's get him out of nappies, short pants, and then Eton before we expect First Honors at University."

William shook his head. "No, my love, I believe our son is more intelligent than any other babes at this age."

She had no intention of arguing with her husband. She was merely happy that he spent time with the child, which was not something her own father had done. She barely saw him until it was time to marry, then he presented himself at her home in Bath and announced she was to have a year with a finishing governess and then make her curtsy to the Queen. After that, she was to enter the marriage mart and find a husband.

She'd been terrified and cried herself to sleep for days after Papa had left. Aunt Margaret calmed her by telling her that was exactly what Papa had tried to do for her, but she resisted after Papa disapproved of the man she loved and sent her into the country for a few years.

Amy tried to do it his way and after two excruciating years of stumbling around, spending time searching for potted plants large enough to hide behind, and panicking every time a gentleman asked her to dance, she begged Papa to let her return to Bath with Aunt Margaret. As much as he tried to dissuade her, she cried enough that he gave up and let her return.

To home.

To safety.

Eventually to William.

All was quiet when they returned from the nursery. Charles had appeared ready for his bath and bed, and Mrs. Grover was in a much better frame of mind when she arrived back from the kitchen.

They proceeded to the second floor where they sat in her office connected to their bedchamber. It was supposed to be the lady's bedchamber, but they'd decided at the beginning of their marriage they would share a bed, rather than sleep apart as was the norm for those of their class.

William sent for Filbert and asked him to make sure the

men he'd directed to guard the vicarage got sufficient breaks. His butler then informed them that Mrs. Peters had spent time that morning in the kitchen, annoying Cook, wanting to do things her way. He indicated that Cook was ready to smack Mrs. Peters over the head with one of the chickens they were preparing for luncheon.

Eventually, he said, Cook chased her from the kitchen with a broom, and Mrs. Peters decided to help Mrs. Grover in the nursery.

"Oh, dear," Amy said. "It's a good thing we told her to help Dawson with the gardening starting in the morning. Do you think that will work?"

"I think having her work somewhere in London would work," William said.

She laughed. "She just wants to feel as though she's earning her money, not having it handed to her."

William addressed Filbert. "The weather is still mild, and Dawson could always use the help. Just tell him that she is not to be assigned difficult work." He paused. "And remind him this is only temporary."

With that issue solved, they turned to their notes. "Right now, we have Mr. Reynolds and the unnamed woman from the Inn." Amy tapped her lips with her pen. "We're not even sure she lives in the village. As I've said, she was someone new to me."

William stretched out in his chair, crossing his ankles and linking his fingers over his middle. "We are assuming the murderer is a villager. Aside from the idea that it was a robbery gone sour, it is quite possible someone came to the vicarage from elsewhere for the sole purpose of killing Mr. Smythe."

"Yes. That is a good point. Which means, in order to solve this and make the villagers feel safe, we need to investigate Mr. Smythe's background."

William stood and reached out his hand to Amy. "Let's dress

for dinner and then retire to the library for a drink or two with the others as they arrive."

They had just taken a sip of their drinks when the front door opened, and the sound of Papa's booming voice echoed at the front entrance.

"Papa, I wasn't expecting you. What a lovely surprise," Amy said as he entered the room and kissed her on the cheek. "What brings you here?"

"To be near my grandchildren, of course. I plan to stay for a while and visit with them."

Amy tried very hard not to let the smile on her lips fade. It probably didn't work.

7

*W*illiam received word the next morning that the so-called coroner would arrive that day. The telegram stated that since it was a long ride from Reading to Wethington Manor, Mr. Mackay assumed he would be able to spend the night before traveling back.

After reading it to Amy, William sighed and tossed the telegram on his desk. "It is not a long ride, merely a couple of hours, but I guess riding here, doing his work, and then riding back might be a lot for one day. We might as well hang out a sign that says 'Hotel Wethington.'"

Amy laughed. "I am afraid I am growing close to panic myself. Aunt Margaret,—not in the best of moods—your parents, Papa, and now Mr. Mackay are slowly turning our home into a hotel. Of course, I would never deprive family of a place to stay and visit, but after rattling around this large Manor since we arrived from Bath, just hearing other voices all the time is a tad disconcerting."

"And don't forget Mrs. Peters." William ran his hand down his face. "I just heard from Dawson this morning that she was getting in his way and offering advice on how he could do things better."

"Did you send the missive to the bishop?"

"Yes. The day after Mr. Smythe was found. No answer back yet, but I'm hoping it won't take long. Of course, we can't do anything until the coroner arrives anyway."

Filbert entered the library and coughed. "My lord, there is a situation that has arisen in the garden."

William rubbed his eyes with his index finger and thumb. "Matters of the house are your jurisdiction, Amy. I'll wait here, and you can tell me what the issue was." He immediately pulled out papers from his top drawer and began to scan the sheets.

Amy walked over to him and pulled the papers from his hand. "My lord, this is the bill from my modiste which you paid weeks ago." She pointed to the scrawl across the page. "Paid."

He leaned back in his chair. "Please, my love, you are much better at handling distressed women than I am."

She narrowed her eyes at him and left the room.

He had about five minutes of peace before Amy returned to the library holding a very dirty, wiggling creature in her hands, her arms extended from her body.

"What the devil is that?"

"A dog."

"A dog? It looks like a filthy rat. Was this the disturbance in the garden?"

"Give me a minute to explain. I shall be right back. I'm having Mrs. Peters clean him up." She raced from the room before he could insist on hearing why Mrs. Peters was going to clean him up.

His life was collapsing. Before he had a chance to dwell too much on that, Amy returned to the room.

"To answer your question, yes, this was the disturbance in the garden." She took a deep breath and settled in the chair in front of his desk. "Mrs. Peters found the dog, and Dawson wanted to whack it over the head and toss it. I dread to think he has done that before." She shuddered.

"No need to go any further," William said. "Mrs. Peters was appalled and insisted on keeping it."

"Yes."

"As long as it doesn't stay here."

Amy shook her head. "No. Mrs. Peters said she would take it home."

Filbert appeared at the door again. "My lord, a Mr. Mackay is here, asking for you."

William stood and walked around the desk. "Let's go speak to this man who the Magistrate said was the closest thing that he had to a coroner."

Mr. Mackay must have been the Magistrate's brother—older brother. He was slightly bent over with a tad more hair, but with the same glassy eyes.

William stuck out his hand. "Mr. Mackay? I am Lord Wethington, and this is my wife, Lady Wethington."

The man nodded and said, "Well, lad, no need to waste time. Where's the body?"

Startled at his abruptness, William said, "It's at the vicarage. Did you arrive in a carriage?"

"Aye, no' a comfortable ride. Must be older than me." He grinned, and William assumed he was making a joke. "I sent it back since Sir Archibald needed it. I'll use your carriage when I return tomorrow."

Appalled at the Magistrate's assumptions but rather than comment on that, William turned to Amy. "Are you ready to go now?"

"Yes. Just let me get my bonnet and cape."

William turned to his butler. "Filbert, can you have the carriage brought around?"

William led Mr. Mackay into the drawing room. Realizing the man had just taken a two-hour trip, good manners declared he should offer the man refreshments before they went to view the body. "Would you care for tea before we go to the vicarage?"

The man waved at him. "Nay, lad. Would rather get this over with. I'll look forward to luncheon when we get back."

Amy arrived back about ten minutes before Filbert announced the carriage was ready. They proceeded out the door and climbed into the vehicle.

It was a short and quiet ride.

Once they arrived at the vicarage, William placed his hand over Amy's. "Perhaps you should wait here. I'm sure after two days the smell in the vicarage will not be pleasant."

"Actually, my stomach has been troubling me of late, so this is one time I don't wish to look at the dead body."

William and Mr. Mackay approached the vicarage. Lyons, one of William's footmen, stood in front of the door. "Good morning, my lord."

"Good morning, Lyons. I assume all is well, and no one has tried to enter the house?"

"No, my lord. I have been here since six this morning, and Carter, who stood the night, said the same thing. Quiet."

William nodded. "You may go back to the Manor. With Mr. Mackay, who was sent here from the Magistrate to view the body and make a report, I will have someone notify Mr. Graves to pick up the vicar's body since I've been told Graves prepares bodies for burial."

It was an odd name for a man who took care of dead bodies and prepared them to be put into a grave. Just one more strange thing about this situation.

He realized as they opened the door and stepped inside that the bishop needed to provide Mr. Smythe's family members with the sad news of Mr. Smythe's demise. He would send a telegram this afternoon.

He was correct. The smell in the house was not pleasant. He

took out a handkerchief to cover his nose. Mr. Mackay seemed oblivious to the odor. Perhaps one's sense of smell diminished with age.

The man shuffled over to where the vicar lay on the floor, his eyes open in surprise, a hole in the center of his chest where the bullet had entered. Mr. Mackay took a minute or so to kneel and touched his fingers to the man's neck. "No pulse."

William rolled his eyes.

The coroner then leaned as close as he could to the bullet hole and looked at it. "The mon was shot."

William ran his hand down his face. "Can you determine when he died?"

Mr. Mackay climbed to his feet, moaning as he stood. "Oh, I'd say a day or two." He dusted his hands then walked over to William. "I'll do my report. Is it time for luncheon yet?"

He should not be surprised, but he was. "Is that all you're going to do?"

"No' much to do. The mon's dead. Can't tell us anything now, can he?" He lumbered past William and headed for the door.

William followed, and they climbed into the carriage. When Amy opened her mouth to ask a question, he shook his head. He preferred to tell her about the outlandish visit to the vicarage in private.

As they proceeded, Mr. Mackay tapped a cadence on his knee that only he could hear, looking out the window, humming to himself.

William cleared his throat. "Will Sir Archibald send someone to investigate?"

He cupped his ear with his hand. "What?"

"I said will Sir Archibald send someone to investigate?"

"Well, I donna ken about that, lad. We're busy this time of the year."

"Busy? Are there certain times of the year more crime

ridden than others? Wouldn't you say that a murder should take precedence over other crimes?"

The coroner rubbed his chin with his hand. "I couldn't say."

Realizing he was only making himself angrier, William ignored the man for the rest of the way. Amy remained silent, but he caught a slight grin on her face. Apparently, she understood how frustrated he was.

Once the carriage came to a stop, he hopped out and helped Amy. He looked at Mr. Mackay. "I have business to attend to, so my driver will see you to the door. My butler will direct you to the drawing room while you await luncheon."

He grabbed Amy's elbow and practically dragged her to the house. He had to get away from the man before he popped him in the jaw. Of all the incompetent individuals he'd met in his life, Mr. Mackay was certainly at the very top of the list.

Before they reached the door, they met Mrs. Peters walking the creature he'd seen before in Amy's hands on a piece of rope. At least the animal was clean.

"Good day, my lord." She smiled at the animal. "He looks much better after his bath."

Amy knelt. "Oh, you're so sweet." She looked up at William. "Isn't he sweet?"

"Yes, indeed." Unfortunately, he was not an animal person. He barely tolerated Persephone, and when Amy and Eloise were pushing a kitten off on each other last year, he'd been subjected to sneezing fits.

"I will send word to Mr. Graves that he may remove the vicar's body and prepare him for burial. As soon as I hear from the bishop about Mr. Smythe's replacement, I will let you know."

Tears came to Mrs. Peters' eyes, and she nodded. "Thank you, my lord. Will you be saying the prayers over his grave then?"

William was startled, not having given that much thought,

but as Lord of the Estate, the responsibility rested with him. "Yes, I will carry out that duty." He nodded, and they entered the house.

"Filbert, send word to Mr. Graves that he can pick up the vicar's body and prepare him for the funeral." He snapped his fingers. "Oh, and when Mr. Mackay shuffles into the house, put him into the drawing room to wait for luncheon. Then have one of the maids prepare a room for him for the night."

"I could use a small sherry before luncheon. Do you care to join me?" William asked as Amy removed her cape and bonnet and handed them to Filbert.

She smiled at him, her eyes lit with mirth. "It appears you are in need of one, but I will pass."

Once he was settled on the settee near a window in his study, he took a sip of sherry and told Amy about the time spent with Mr. Mackay in the vicarage.

"That is preposterous," Amy said. "You're a member of Parliament. You should write to someone. How can Sir Archibald be allowed to dump this on us with no help whatsoever? A man of the cloth has been murdered!"

"This will definitely be something I will take up with Parliament, but in the meantime, we have a killer out there."

"My lord, my lady, luncheon is served." Filbert stood at the door. "Shall I direct Mr. Mackay to the dining room?"

"Yes, please."

* * *

LADY LILY, Mr. Colbert, Aunt Margaret, and Papa were just seating themselves when she and William arrived. Once they took their seats, Mr. Mackay shuffled in, Filbert leading the way. William gestured to the seat next to his mother.

William looked at the group. "This is Mr. Mackay from the Magistrate's office. He is here to conduct an examination of the vicar's body and deliver a report." William gestured to each person at the table, introducing them.

As soon as food was put in front of the man, he lowered his head, shoveled his meal into his mouth, and never said a word. Eventually, everyone stopped staring at him and enjoyed their luncheon, conversing as they normally did.

"How are you today, Aunt Margaret?" Amy asked between sips of a delicious white soup.

"Actually, Niece, I feel better today. My stomach has not been bothering me of late. I am still a tad fatigued in the afternoon, but a short nap restores me. Perhaps we can take a trip into the village one day this week. I feel the need to walk a bit in the fresh air and visit the shops."

Lady Lily wiped her mouth on her napkin. "That is a wonderful idea. If you don't mind, I'd like to join you."

"Of course," Amy said. "I will ask Mrs. Grover to go with us so we can take Charles. He would love an afternoon stroll in his pram."

She would also use the occasion to talk to shopkeepers and visitors. Just then she realized the next day was Saturday, so the pedlars would be there, as well.

"I suggest we go tomorrow, one of the days the vendors set up. It makes for a much livelier place."

William cleared his throat, and Amy looked over at him. He gestured with his head. Mr. Mackay held his fork and knife in his hands but was sound asleep, getting dangerously close to dropping his head onto his plate.

They all looked at each other. William waved a footman over. "Please awaken our guest and help him to his room. First, you will need to check with the housekeeper to see which chamber has been prepared for him."

Trying very hard to hide his smile, the footman left and was back in a few minutes and tapped Mr. Mackay on the shoulder.

"Sir, I will be happy to escort you to your room so you may have a short lie-down."

The man looked around, apparently confused at first, but then stood, straightened his clothes, bowed to them all, and followed the footman.

"Is that the best the Magistrate could send to conduct a report on the vicar's murder?" Lady Lily asked.

"I'm afraid so. Not only that, but the Magistrate also seemed totally disinterested in the matter."

"That's outrageous," Papa said. He looked at William. "We must take this up with Parliament."

"I intend to, but in the meantime, we have a dead man and no one under arrest."

Papa took a sip of his wine and looked directly at her. "You will not get involved in this, Daughter. You have a household to run and a child to raise."

William turned his attention to Papa. "With all due respect, my lord, my wife has experience and knowledge when it comes to solving crimes. Since it appears the responsibility now rests with me since we are receiving no help from the Magistrate's office, I will depend on her knowledge to resolve this matter. Charles is well taken care of, and we both visit with him throughout the day. Our housekeeper, Mrs. O'Sullivan, who has been with me in Bath and here, runs the house efficiently."

Papa grunted and returned to his food.

Amy smiled and cut a piece of lamb. She'd never appreciated her husband more.

---

8

*T*he next morning, the ladies left for the village about an hour after breakfast. Mr. Mackay had still not made an appearance, and William mentioned that perhaps he planned to stay a while and take a free vacation.

They made quite a parade with the pram and Mrs. Grover along with Amy, Lady Lily, and Aunt Margaret. It was a fine day, another autumn day with pale sun and only a slightly lowered temperature. They were all bundled up, and Amy felt the excitement. Getting out of the Manor was a good idea. They all spent too much time indoors, and soon the cold weather would not allow them much in the way of outside activities.

"Aunt Margaret, you look very fetching today," Amy said. Her aunt wore a lovely deep green suit with a silk beige blouse, topped off with a perky matching hat on her head. Her black leather gloves and buttoned boots finished off the outfit.

"Indeed. I do feel very good."

Lady Lily patted her hand. "That's wonderful. I found with my two pregnancies that once I passed those first three months it was all well until the end."

Amy was pleased to have her familiar Aunt Margaret back. "Perhaps you should visit the dressmaker while we are here. You will most likely require new dresses and gowns in a month or two."

"You are correct, Niece. I had to leave the top button on my skirt undone so I could breathe," she said with a grin.

"Have you secured the services of a midwife yet?" Lady Lily asked.

"Yes. A Mrs. Townsend visited with me at Amy's request just yesterday while she and William were out. She is a lovely lady." She sighed. "Jonathan had wanted to speak with whomever I secured for midwifery services, but we were unable to speak with Mrs. Townsend before he left. I don't know how long my husband will need to straighten out his uncle's estate. I might still be here when the babe arrives."

Amy stepped around some animal leavings and said, "I so wish Dr. Stevens could have attended you, but she is in Bath. She did such a wonderful job with Eloise and me."

Aunt Margaret laughed. "She must have done a wonderful job, delivering three babies at once."

Amy's thoughts returned to the day Charles and his twin cousins all arrived at the same time on the same day. Poor Dr. Stevens had her hands full, running back and forth between the two houses, but it had all turned out well.

The noise of the village reached them before they made it over the slight hill that separated the Manor from the village. "It sounds like a busy day today," Amy said.

"My lady, do you wish to have me stroll along with you, or settle with the pram while you shop?" Mrs. Grover asked.

"It is most likely better if you find a place to rest. Pushing a pram with this crowd of people is not a good idea. I will return occasionally to make sure all is well," Amy said.

The nanny found a bench under a tree, and Amy, Lady Lily, and Aunt Margaret headed to the shops.

Although she enjoyed shopping and would, of course, stop in at the bookstore, Amy planned to gather whatever information she could about Mr. Smythe.

"I'm off to the dressmaker," Aunt Margaret said, heading to the shop with a sign in front of it advertising dressmaking and alterations.

"I really must see about a new hat," Lady Lily said. "Are you here for anything in particular?"

Yes, to solve a murder.

"No, I am in the browsing mood." Happy to be able to gather information by herself, she walked off in the opposite direction from Lady Lily and Aunt Margaret.

With the very first visit she made, she learned that it didn't take much to get information on Mr. Smythe. Every shop owner Amy encountered was more than eager to talk about the vicar and his murder.

Mrs. Baldwin, the woman who owned the laundry where the single men of the village brought their dirty clothes, looked almost too happy to discuss a murder and put aside for a few minutes what had to be a difficult job.

On the pretense of asking about how the laundress's business was faring, Amy casually mentioned Mr. Smythe.

The woman clutched her apron and stared at Amy wide-eyed. "Oh, my goodness, my lady. I was so very distressed when I heard the news that I couldn't work that day. Mr. Smythe was such a wonderful man and gave the most inspiring sermons. Why anyone would be able to look the man in the face and kill him still gives me shivers."

Before she began her search for information, Amy had decided it would not be in their best interest to let the villagers know that she and William were in any way involved in discovering who shot Mr. Smythe. She'd learned from past murders that having friendly conversations revealed a great deal of information when people didn't feel as though they were being interrogated.

If it became known that the Magistrate had little interest in the murder and had shoved it off on her and William, some people would view her with caution, not wishing to discuss the incident. She oftentimes received the best information from those who liked to chatter.

Mrs. Baldwin leaned in close and, looking around the laundry, lowered her voice. "I must admit, my lady, that I don't sleep well since the incident. Who knows what sort of evil is out there, waiting to destroy us all?"

Well, that was certainly an appropriate take on the murder, and until the killer was caught, a very astute one. She patted Mrs. Baldwin's hand. "I'm sure it will be fine."

"Do you know if they caught the culprit yet?"

"I haven't been in touch with the Magistrate since we reported the crime." That was a fine way to answer the question without answering the question.

"Oh, I see. Well, I hope you hear something soon."

Amy thanked her for her time and left the building and headed to the silversmith's.

"Good afternoon, my lady. Are you in search of a piece of fine silver jewelry?"

Mr. Davidson was an older gentleman who was always dressed in formal clothes as if he were attending a ball in Bath or London. Amy assumed he considered his goods above the others and wanted to have himself represented as such.

"Good afternoon to you as well, Mr. Davidson. Actually, I am looking for an ink holder for my husband's desk."

"Ah, I have just the thing." He walked to the back of the store and picked up an item and brought it to her. "This is a lovely piece, my lady. His lordship would be quite pleased with it."

She picked it up and studied it closer. "This is very nice." She sighed and placed it back on the counter.

"Is something the matter, my lady?"

Amy shook her head and sighed again. "Nothing, Mr. Davidson. I am just unable to make any decisions since I heard about poor Mr. Smythe."

The silversmith sucked in a deep breath. "I know. Isn't that troublesome? The man was so young. And so very popular."

"Yes, indeed. Everyone loved him."

Mr. Davidson took a cloth from a small pile next to him and began to rub the inkwell. "Understand, please, that I do not wish to cast aspersions, but not *everyone* loved the vicar."

Amy's heartbeat sped up, but she put on her best surprised expression. "Is that so? I thought Mr. Smythe was quite popular."

Mr. Davidson sniffed and continued to rub the inkwell. "Mr. Granger was certainly not fond of the man."

"Indeed?"

Just then the bell over the door to the shop chimed, and a very young woman and an older man entered the shop. Amy recognized her as the woman who was crying in the Inn the day she and Eloise had seen her with Mr. Smythe.

Mr. Davidson immediately moved toward the couple. "Please excuse me for one minute." He looked back at Amy. "I will be more than happy to wrap that inkwell up for you."

It would be in her best interests to have more time with the man without anyone else in the shop. "I will think about it, Mr. Davidson. It certainly is lovely, but as I said, I am finding it hard to make decisions right now."

"Very well, my lady. I look forward to speaking with you again."

Amy took her time looking around the shop as Mr. Davidson gave his attention to the couple who apparently were looking to sell something rather than buy.

It would be quite odd for her to remain in the store just so she could hear the conversation, so she left having more questions than when she had entered.

Feeling a bit hungry with all the wonderful smells coming from pedlars selling savory pies and grilled meats, she decided to look around for Lady Lily and Aunt Margaret to gather them all to have lunch at the Inn. She hoped they would not be ready to leave because she still needed to buy a few things and maybe get a bit more information.

She had stopped a few times to see about Charles and told Mrs. Grover the last time she saw her that it would be best for her to return to the Manor with Charles so she could feed him his luncheon and put him down for his nap.

Lady Lily left the cobbler's shop just as Amy approached it. Her mother-in-law hurried up to her. "Mr. Colbert refuses to purchase new shoes even though he is in dire need of a new pair." She laughed. "So last week I brought a pair of his shoes here, and the cobbler did a drawing of them. I was just inquiring when they would be ready."

"That's a wonderful idea, my lady. I'm sure Mr. Colbert would be quite pleased. I think in most cases, men would never purchase things for themselves without our help." She linked arms with her and said, "Do you have any idea where Lady Margaret is?"

"I have seen her on and off since we've been here, but it's been about twenty minutes since I saw her last." Lady Lily pointed toward one of the shops. "There she is."

Amy was stunned to find Aunt Margaret leaving the village store that sold baby clothing, toys, furniture, and anything a little baby was in need of. Could it be her aunt was taking this whole thing seriously? She thought the day would never come when Aunt Margaret was a mother. Of course, she mothered her once her own mother died, but Amy was ten years by that time. She shook her head in amazement.

Aunt Margaret saw them before they were able to reach her, and she hurried in their direction. "I hope you both plan to have luncheon because I am quite hungry."

"We are, but I would like to sit down after being on my feet. We were considering the Inn rather than one of the vendors."

"Yes. I agree," Aunt Margaret said.

They made their way to the Inn and found it quite crowded but were able to find a small table near the front of the room. Lucy, the innkeeper's daughter, arrived at their table with three mugs of ale. As usual with the girl, she wore a bright smile. "I just love vendor day; we are so very busy with all the people who do not wish to eat and walk."

"That sounds like us," Amy said, returning the girl's smile. "What is your specialty today?"

"Baked salmon in some type of sauce. I am never sure what my da uses for these sauces, but everyone likes them. We also have mutton and chops."

Once they placed their orders, Amy remembered that young Lucy could be a great source of information since most villagers have been at the Inn more than once. She would have overheard conversations that might be helpful.

Lucy brought warm bread and crock of butter to them, then she stopped at two tables that had been vacated by the patrons and cleaned off the tables, stacking the dishes in such a way that Amy held her breath until the girl made it to the counter in front of the door that led to the kitchen.

"That serving girl is amazing at being able to handle so many duties," Lady Lily said.

Amy took a sip of ale and said, "Lucy has been working here since she was about eleven years. Her father owns the Inn, and she and her three brothers are kept quite busy."

"My, such a young age to take on duties like that, but I guess in small villages like this, it's important for families to help each other."

"And what makes it hard for Lucy is her mother died when she was a mere baby, so she's had no female influence."

Lady Lily delicately smeared a tab of butter onto a piece of bread. "Yet she seems quite cheerful."

Just then the girl they spoke of arrived at their table, balancing three plates of food. She set them down in front of them, wiping her fingers on her apron. "Is there anything else I can bring you? More ale, perhaps?"

"Not for me." Amy looked at the other two. "Do either of you want more?"

Both ladies declined, but Lady Lily asked for tea once they finished their meal.

"I have been so busy walking around and checking on Charles that I haven't had a chance to really look at things," Amy said. "Are you up for more shopping?"

Lady Lily and Aunt Margaret both shook their heads. "After this wonderful luncheon, I am ready for a nap," Aunt Margaret said.

Amy remembered how much she enjoyed a nap in the afternoons when she was pregnant with Charles.

"I agree with Lady Margaret," Lady Lily said. "I might just take a nap myself even though I don't have the same excuse." She smiled warmly at Aunt Margaret.

"Then I shall remain for a while. I don't expect to be more than another half hour or so."

They parted ways outside the Inn. Amy addressed the items on her shopping list and once she'd obtained what she needed, she headed to the Manor. Any attempts to gather more information hadn't worked because all the shopkeepers were busy with the crowds.

She decided then that she would take a trip to the village one afternoon next week and speak with Lucy. She could be very helpful in gathering information on the villagers.

As she came down the small hill a short distance from the

Manor, she was surprised to see William walking in her direction. They met up near the stables behind the icehouse.

"Were you coming to seek me?" Amy asked.

William ran his fingers through his hair. "Indeed. There is news I wanted to pass along to you and thought away from the Manor would be best."

Amy's brows rose. "Indeed? And what is that? Is all well?" She gripped his arm. "Charles!"

"No. No. Nothing like that." He released her hand and took her arm as they walked toward the house. "I received a telegram today from the Magistrate." He stopped and looked off into the distance. "He has decided to allow Mr. Mackay to remain here and conduct the investigation into the vicar's death."

Amy just stared at him, horrified. "What? Mr. Mackay is useless."

"Even more useless than you think."

Amy narrowed her eyes. "What do you mean?"

"The doctor just left. Mr. Mackay has developed an *ague* and must remain in bed for at least a couple of weeks."

9

"Mr. Mackay is staying here to solve the mystery of the vicar's death when he offered no advice or meaningful insight when he viewed the body? And now he is lying in bed, sick with an *ague*?"

"You are quick, Amy. That is the gist of it."

"This is becoming a nightmare." She shook her head. "The only benefit I can see in this is he won't be stumbling around trying to solve a murder and getting in our way. But he will need to have his meals brought to him. Someone must be assigned to care for him. Can we spare one of the maids for that responsibility?"

"No. Remember we already have four other guests the staff is dealing with. My thoughts are to find a woman in the village who might take up the duty. There must be someone who could use the money."

Amy tapped her lips with her finger. "I'm thinking that perhaps Mrs. Elliot might consider it. I heard not too long ago that her daughter married and moved to Scotland. Since Mrs. Elliot has lived here her entire life, she chose not to go with her daughter. I can speak with her. I think the two women supported themselves by taking in sewing, but with only her left, she might find the position agreeable."

They arrived at the house. Papa jumped up from where he was sitting in the drawing room and approached her at the entrance hall. "Where have you been all day, Daughter?"

To say she was startled did not fully explain it. "I was in the village with Aunt Margaret and Lady Lily."

"They returned hours ago."

She removed her bonnet and handed it to Filbert at the door. "I had some things I needed to purchase."

It suddenly occurred to her that he was questioning her as if she were a child. "Is there a reason you were so concerned with my whereabouts?"

"Well, yes. I thought we might spend some time together."

William made a quick exit from the entrance hall to his library. Amy's eyes narrowed at her husband's desertion.

She turned her attention back to her father. As far back as she could remember, Papa had never uttered those words to her. He was a businessman with a heavy schedule. In fact, they only saw each other a few times a year when she was growing up because she and Aunt Margaret lived in Bath and he and her brother Michael lived in London.

She walked into the drawing room and sat. "I was about to send for tea. Would you care to join me?"

"Yes." He rubbed his hands. "Tea sounds fine. I will have a glass of whisky."

Amy stepped out of the drawing room and asked Filbert to have tea sent in along with a bottle of whisky. After settling in her chair again, she folded her hands in her lap and looked over at Papa. He glanced back at her.

"How was your trip to the village?"

"Very nice. I like going on the days of the week when the vendors are there."

"Very crowded I imagine."

"Yes."

Silence.

He cleared his throat. "How is Charles?"

"Very well, thank you. Mrs. Grover joined us for a while, and then I asked her to return home for Charles' luncheon and nap."

Papa nodded. He shifted in his chair and crossed one leg over the other. "The weather was nice for a stroll in the village today."

Amy nodded.

Silence.

She breathed a sigh of relief when one of the footmen entered the room, pushing a tea cart. A flowered teapot, two cups, two saucers, a plate of biscuits, and a glass with a bottle of whisky.

Papa hopped up and poured himself a glass of whisky and settled back down again. She fixed her tea and offered him the plate of cookies. He shook his head no.

Amy sipped her tea and looked out the window.

Silence.

"You should take a walk to the village sometime, Papa. There are various stores and shops you might be interested in."

He waved his hand. "Strolling around a village is not something that appeals to me."

She sighed and sipped more tea. "Michael and Eloise do not live far from here. You said when you arrived that you wanted to spend time with your grandchildren. You know there are two of them there."

"Yes. That is my plan. I thought tomorrow to ride over to Michael's place and talk a bit about our business and then see his daughters."

She placed her cup in the saucer. "Is it your plan to retire from your businesses with Michael?"

"I have been considering it. I've given more of the responsibility to him, and he is doing a fine job of it." He downed the rest of his whisky and stood. "I believe I will visit with William for a while." With a nod, he left the room, leaving Amy with a sense of relief and sympathy for her husband.

* * *

THE NEXT DAY BEING SUNDAY, William had decided it was perfect to hold the funeral for Mr. Smythe. Mr. Graves had notified him the day before that Mr. Smythe was ready for burial.

The villagers were used to attending church on Sunday, so William expected a good showing for the man.

Once he entered the church and stepped up to the chancel, he determined that he'd been right. It appeared most of the village was in church. He had prepared a eulogy for the man, but he had little to go on, other than the few months he had been with the Church of St. Agatha. He'd taken the time yesterday to speak with some of the villagers to get information that he might use in his tribute to Mr. Smythe.

He faced the congregation and cleared his throat. Luckily, he had given speeches in Parliament, so speaking to the crowd was not a daunting task.

During his talk, he saw many women dabbing at their eyes. Mr. Smythe had been a popular man. Which made it even more difficult to figure out who killed him. William had thought about a random act; someone robbing the vicarage and Mr. Smythe coming in at the wrong time.

When he spoke with the few people about the vicar, he asked each one if they heard the shot that killed the man. No one had heard it, and no one could offer information on why the very well-liked man of the cloth had been killed.

Following the eulogy, then the interment, the villagers gathered at the Fellowship Hall alongside the church. The women all brought food to be shared by everyone. William had provided the staff to assist and various beverages to go along with the fare.

Amy sat alongside William, across from his parents, Lady Margaret, and his father-in-law, Franklin. "There are a few things I have to share with you when we return home. With so many people around us all the time, it is difficult," she said in a lowered voice.

"It is easy enough. Just announce when we return home that we are visiting with Charles for a few hours." He laughed. "That should keep them away for a while."

"I don't know. When we were at the village yesterday, Aunt Margaret spent some time in a store that sells only baby items."

"Indeed?"

"Yes. And it seems her troubles with nausea have ceased and she is feeling—and behaving—more like the Aunt Margaret I've known all my life."

"I am glad to hear it." He looked across from them where Lady Margaret was conversing with his mother and said, "She is not completely herself. Did you notice she is wearing two different gloves?"

"Oh, my goodness, she is looking like me. Except I do remember to find the correct shoes when I leave the house now."

"But you are wearing your hat backward."

"I am not, William. This is the way the hat is supposed to be worn. You just do not understand female fashion."

He removed the blue hat with a bird perched on top and handed it to her. She glared at him and checked the inside of the brim. He was correct; she had the thing on backward.

She replaced it—correctly—and ignored him and his chuckle while she finished her food.

Lady Margaret stood and shook out her skirts. "I am ready for a nap."

That seemed to be the signal for the rest of their group to stand. Franklin offered his arm to his sister and made his way to the door, followed by William's parents and him and Amy.

They managed to squeeze into the carriage since it was a short ride. As planned, William announced when they arrived home that he and Amy would be spending time in the nursery with their son.

After dismissing Mrs. Grover for a couple of hours, they did, in fact, enjoy playing with him. Holding him up to stand on his feet. He laughed and jumped up and down while Amy held his chubby hands in hers.

"He will be walking soon," William said.

They read him a book that he attempted to chew and crawled around the carpet chasing a ball that William dangled in front of him.

"One thing I wanted to tell you," Amy said. "When I was in the silversmith's store yesterday, I brought up the subject of Mr. Smythe and how well loved he was." She removed her son's hand from the back of her hair that he had in quite a grip. "Mr. Davidson mentioned that Mr. Granger had a problem with Mr. Smythe. If I remember correctly, he said something like Mr. Granger wasn't so fond of the vicar."

"Hmm." William dangled his watch in front of Charles. "Have we started keeping a list?"

"I believe so, although up until now we only had Mr. Reynolds on it, who had the run in with the vicar over him marrying his daughter to the farmer without permission."

"Quite a short list."

"We can get additional information about Mr. Granger if we go together to the village." She paused as Charles crawled over to the small rocking chair in his room, pulled himself up, and took two steps before falling on his bum.

"Did you see that?" William said. "I tell you, this is a very intelligent lad."

Amy rose from the floor and picked her son up who had gone from surprised to tears. She cuddled him and said, "I would also like to speak with Lucy at the Inn. She is there all the time, and she might know who the young lady was who was in a corner crying with Mr. Smythe attempting to sooth her. And—that same woman was the one who entered the silversmith's shop with an older man, interrupting my conversation with Mr. Davidson right after he mentioned Mr. Granger."

William reached out and took Charles from Amy's arms. The lad had settled down and looked as though he was ready for another nap. "We should probably summon Mrs. Grover and have her give Charles his bath and dinner."

Amy stood. "I will do it. Then I'll be in my office, making up our list."

* * *

THE NEXT AFTERNOON, Amy and William set out for the village. She kept herself busy all morning with the housekeeper, Mrs. O'Sullivan, and Cook, going over the menus and other issues that needed her attention while William did some work on his ledgers. They didn't join the others for luncheon since they intended to speak with Lucy at the Inn.

Since it appeared as though it might rain at any time, they took the carriage for the short ride.

"Have you heard anything from the bishop?" she asked as the carriage rolled forward.

"Yes. In fact, I received a missive from his office this morning. He sent his regrets over the death of Mr. Smythe and indicated a new vicar will be arriving sometime this week."

"That is good news. I hope this one is as pleasant as Mr. Smythe." Amy paused for a minute, admiring the colorful leaves on the trees with autumn doing its usual work. "If there is a new vicar coming this week, I think it might be a good idea for me to go to the vicarage and clear out Mr. Smythe's things. We should also let Mrs. Peters know that her job will soon resume."

"Thank goodness," William mumbled.

"And while we're here, we must visit with Mrs. Elliot and inquire about her taking over the care of Mr. Mackay. Mrs. O'Sullivan nicely mentioned that with Margie taking on the responsibility for Mr. Mackay they were short of help."

"It appears we have quite a bit to do in the village today."

"As much as I enjoy going to the village on vendor days, I am glad we won't have to deal with crowds today. Things will be peaceful, and we will be able to get more done. And Lucy won't be running around in the Inn ale room trying to keep up with orders."

William looked out the window and then turned back to her. "Do you have Mrs. Elliot's direction?"

"Yes. Mrs. O'Sullivan had the information. She apparently used Mrs. Elliot's services when she needed some sewing done."

"Then it appears we are all set."

It was drizzling when they emerged from the carriage. They decided to have luncheon first at the Inn. The added advantage of the rain made for an even quieter place.

"My goodness, you are back so soon?" Lucy asked as Amy and William took seats closer to the window where the light was better. The warmth from the fireplace helped to take the damp chill from the air.

"I just cannot stay away," Amy said.

They ordered the mutton stew and were immediately served warm bread and butter, along with a dish of jellied eels that Amy asked Lucy to remove. She shivered as the girl walked off. "How can anyone eat those?"

Since the Inn was only half full, Amy engaged Lucy in

conversation when she arrived with their mutton. "Were you able to have time off for Mr. Smythe's funeral yesterday morning?"

The girl picked up dishes from the table next to them and balanced them on her arm. "Yes. But I had duties here, so I was only able to listen to part of your eulogy, my lord. It was lovely. It made it quite hard to return from that lovely service and listen to Mr. Reynolds disparage dear Mr. Smythe."

"Yes, he apparently had a quarrel with him," William said.

"A quarrel is one thing, but he sat here and drank his ale, pounding the table and saying over and over how he was glad the man was dead." She shifted the plates in her hands. "He grew quite belligerent until Da threw him out."

"He's happy the man is dead?" Amy said.

William shrugged. "Just because someone is happy that another is deceased doesn't mean he is the one who caused it." He picked up his spoon and dipped it into the mutton stew. "But I believe Mr. Reynolds is definitely someone to keep on our list."

Once they finished, a man she'd never seen before approached their table. "Excuse me, my lord, my lady. I overheard the young serving girl address you. Do you mind if I sit?"

William glanced at Amy and when she nodded, he said, "Yes, please do. I am Lord Wethington, and this is my wife, Lady Wethington."

"It is truly a pleasure to meet you. I am Mr. Kenneth Walsh, third son of Lord Maurice Lawton, recently of Bristol."

"Lawton? An earl if I am correct," William said.

"Yes, that is so."

William leaned back in his chair, crossing his arms over his chest. "What brings you here to our little village?"

"I recently left my home in Bristol and purchased one here in Wethingford. Renovations are being made before I move in.

I've always admired this village and now that I am free to live wherever I wish, I decided to settle here."

"Has something changed that now you can live where you wish?" Amy asked.

He hesitated for a moment. "Yes. I am an artist and lived in both London and Bristol. It was easier there to sell my work to distinguished art galleries. I have decided to retire and just do my painting for enjoyment."

"I think you will be happy here," William said.

They chatted pleasantly for a few more minutes, and then Amy and William left, deciding that with Lucy being so busy and unable to speak with them and the weather so dreadful, they would cut short their trek around the village.

10

*A*my had hoped to question Lucy about the woman who was crying in the Inn, but the girl had been summoned by her da who had her washing dishes in between serving customers, so there was no opportunity to do so.

"That poor girl certainly has a great deal of duties. I hope she receives at least a little bit of coin for her work," William said as they headed to the carriage.

It had begun to rain quite heavily, and they'd decided it was better to go directly from the Inn to Mrs. Elliot's house, and then home to a warm drink in front of a comfortable fire. Preferably in their bedchamber so they could have some peace and quiet.

"I would be surprised if she did receive anything for her efforts. Generally, when a family owns a business, everyone is expected to work for the roof over their heads and the food in their bellies," Amy said.

"Hopefully, she will marry one day, and her husband will provide for her."

The carriage left the shops area and went farther north to a section where several cottages were clustered together.

William looked at the paper in his hand and tapped on the ceiling for Benson to stop.

"Are you sure you don't wish to wait here?" William said as he moved to get out of the carriage. "The rain is quite heavy."

"No. I think Mrs. Elliot would feel more comfortable if I were with you."

"Very well." He stepped out, opened the umbrella, and helped Amy down the few steps from the carriage. "Be careful, it is slippery out here."

They hurried to the door and knocked. It was opened within minutes. "My lord, my lady! What a surprise to see you here. If you need something, you should have sent a staff member to summon me."

Obviously flustered and then suddenly remembering her manners, Mrs. Elliot stepped back. "Please, come in out of that nasty weather."

Mrs. Elliot appeared to be in her forties. She was a very pretty woman with blonde hair and deep blue eyes. Despite a wrinkle or two on her face, she maintained an aura of youthfulness. Amy had always found her cheerful and caring when they'd met in the village and at church.

The cottage was small and comfortable. The furniture worn but clean. One side of the space held a table and two chairs, and a door on the other side opened into a bedroom. A small fire burned in the fireplace, taking the edge off the dampness.

"I am so sorry to be unprepared, my lord, but I can offer you tea and some biscuits."

Amy sensed the poor woman's embarrassment at their appearing at her door when she was not expecting them. Attempting to put the woman at ease, Amy said, "Please do not be upset. We have just come from the Inn where we had luncheon, so tea and biscuits, while greatly appreciated, are not necessary."

Mrs. Elliot continued to flutter and pointed to the settee

and two chairs that made a small grouping near the fireplace. "Won't you please have a seat and tell me what I can do for you."

Once they were settled, William cleared his throat. "The reason we are here, Mrs. Elliot, is to offer you a temporary position at the Manor."

Her brows rose and a slight flush appeared on her cheeks. "What is that my lord?"

"We have a guest staying at the Manor who has developed an *ague*. He needs someone to care for him, doing the usual things one does for a sick person. He is elderly, and I assume it will take him some time to recover. Would you be interested in helping us out? We offer you the same wage we pay our other servants."

"We don't wish to interfere with your sewing business, however," Amy quickly said.

Mrs. Elliot smiled. "I'm afraid with Donna married and off to her husband's home in Scotland, I am unable to keep up with the requests, so I am slowly losing customers."

"This position is not permanent, but if you would be willing to move into the Manor, we can provide a room and meals. When Mr. Mackay has recovered, we would assist you in finding something permanent."

The woman burst into tears. "That is so helpful, my lord. I have been so worried since Donna married. This house is rented, and the last two months I have been unable to make a full payment, so I am sure Mr. Devins will ask me to find other accommodations soon."

"Well, it is settled then. If you wish to pack up your things, we will have a carriage sent this afternoon. Do you need the use of a wagon, also? To bring your furniture with you? We can store it for you," William said.

She shook her head. "No. Most of this belongs to Mr. Devins. Things that belonged to me I sent along with Donna."

She smiled. "To give her a sense of home while she adjusts to her new life."

"That was quite generous of you."

Mrs. Elliot smiled softly. "My only child. She tried very hard to get me to move with them, but I didn't think that was a good idea. I love it here in Wethingford, having been here all my life. Also, this was an arranged match and very advantageous for her, so I wanted her to be able to adjust to her husband and new home without me hovering over her."

"Very wise," William said.

Amy and William rose. "Then it is settled. We will send a carriage around. Will five o'clock be sufficient time for you?"

Mrs. Elliot looked at the blue flowered clock on the mantel. "Yes. That is fine. I will get started immediately."

"That went quite easy," Amy said as the carriage headed toward the Manor. "I had heard she wasn't doing too well with Donna gone, but she seemed delighted to accept our offer."

"I would say from what she told us that she would have been in quite a pickle if we hadn't come along." William shifted in his seat. "We must find something for her at the Manor once Mr. Mackay is up and about again."

Amy laughed. "Do you think that day will arrive? As we pointed out, he is elderly and right now he is living better than he probably has his entire life. No work to do, no bodies to declare dead, three meals a day, a lovely room to convalesce in. I don't think his recovery will be quick."

William sighed. "I believe you are correct. We also need to inform Mrs. Peters that as soon as we clear the Vicarage out, she can return to her duties."

"I suggest we pay her for the rest of the week and tell her she can go home now and prepare for the new vicar's arrival."

"Yes. Send her home, please. Mrs. O'Sullivan was the last person who told me of Mrs. Peters' interference in her duties."

Amy patted his hand. "We shall tell her today. Let's hope Mrs. Elliot is not like Mrs. Peters. Somehow, I don't believe so."

* * *

MRS. ELLIOT ARRIVED AT FIVE-THIRTY, smiling and eager to take on her duties. She thanked Amy and William again and wanted to immediately begin her work.

"I think it's a better idea to settle into your room and then join us for dinner. It will make it easier to introduce you to everyone at once." Amy joined arms with her and moved her up the stairs. "The patient is now eating dinner in his room, so once our dinner is finished, I can introduce Mr. Mackay to you, and you may start tomorrow."

"Oh, my lady, I feel as though I should not be having my dinner with you. I am an employee. I should dine with the staff."

They reached the top of the stairs, and Amy led her to the room that had been prepared for her. "The staff has already dined, and there will be no concern over you dining with us. We are not at all formal in the country."

Mrs. Elliot also felt the room they gave her was much too nice for an employee, but Amy pointed out that this room was next to Mr. Mackay's, and it would be more convenient for her to be near him.

"If you go back down the stairs, ask Filbert at the door where the library is. We gather there before dinner."

"What time, my lady?"

"Dinner is at seven, so we generally gather around six-thirty. That should give you time to unpack."

With all of that taken care of, and after taking a quick wash and changing her gown for dinner, Amy joined William in the library where he was sitting at his desk, scratching away on a piece of vellum.

She walked around the desk and sat her hip on the chair armrest. "What are you so diligently doing?"

William leaned back in the chair and wrapped his arm around her waist. "I'm looking at what we have so far with the vicar's murder. Right now, we have only one suspect, Mr. Reynolds. We have the possibility of the woman crying in the Inn and Mr. Granger who we really know nothing about, except Mr. Davidson seemed to think he was another person not unhappy with the vicar's demise."

"I was hoping to pry information out of Lucy about the unknown woman, but she is certainly a hard one to speak with."

William laughed. "I foresee many meals in the future at the Inn. How is Mrs. Elliot settling in?"

"It appeared she didn't bring much with her. I can't imagine what would have happened to her if we had not needed someone to take care of Mr. Mackay."

"Rosebud, come back here." The small scruffy dog that Mrs. Peters had rescued raced into the room, running around the chairs, enjoying a good sprint. Mrs. Peters trotted after her. Persephone, who had been enjoying a nap near the fireplace, stood, shook herself off, growled at the animal, and walked from the room.

Mrs. Peters made a dive for the dog, missed her, but landed on her shoulder. She immediately cried out with pain. Amy jumped up and ran to her while William took on the chore of catching the dog. Having more luck than Mrs. Peters, he held the animal by the scruff of her neck.

"Why is this animal still here?"

Amy helped Mrs. Peters off the floor. "Are you injured?"

"I believe I bruised my shoulder, my lady." She rubbed the spot and looked over at William holding the dog. "Rosebud, you are a bad dog."

"Rosebud?"

"Yes, my lady. That is the name I gave her." She still rubbed her shoulder.

"Mrs. Peters, if you see Mrs. O'Sullivan, I am sure she has an ointment you can use to help the pain. Also, we have received word that the new vicar will be arriving shortly. His lordship and I will be going through Mr. Smythe's files and sorting out anything that should go back to the bishop. Once we are finished, you will be able to prepare the vicarage for the new man."

"That is very good news, indeed."

William walked across the room and plopped the dog into Mrs. Peters' arms. "Since I know you will be busy preparing for the new vicar, I insist that you take the time to do what you need to do. We will, of course, pay you for your time until the new man arrives."

"Oh, thank you so much, my lord. You are quite generous."

"If you wish to gather whatever you need to, I will have Filbert arrange to have the carriage brought around." He smiled at her as she made to leave the room, still rubbing her shoulder. "Oh, Mrs. Peters, be sure to bring your dog with you."

William walked to the sideboard and poured a whisky. "Sweetheart, would you care for a sherry?"

"Yes, I would."

With drinks in their hands, they sat on the settee side by side. "I thought moving to the country would make our lives simpler and quieter," William said. "It seems we simply attract chaos."

Just then Mrs. Grover brought Charles in for a visit before his bedtime. Amy laid her glass aside and held out her arms. The baby smiled and reached for her.

"Be careful, my lady; he's been drooling all day."

"Of course, he is. He's getting some teeth." She looked at William. "Look, isn't this a new one?" She pointed to a small stub alongside his left front tooth.

"I believe it is."

Her husband grinned like the lad had already taken Firsts at University. She didn't have the heart to tell him all babies at his age had teeth popping up all the time.

After playing with Charles as if he were their favorite toy—which he was—Mrs. Grover took him away to put to bed. Amy had tried once before reading a book to him before he slept, but he was more interested in pulling at it, chewing it, and smacking it with his little hand. Once he was a tad older, she would do that, remembering her mother reading to her before bedtime each night.

Just then Aunt Margaret, Papa, and the Colberts entered the room. Once drinks were in everyone's hands, they all took seats. Lady Lily had a story to tell about her conversation with Mrs. Peters who told her the new vicar was arriving soon and she would be preparing for his arrival, so if there was anything Lady Lily needed her to do, it would have to be soon.

What made the story funny was Lady Lily had never asked Mrs. Peters to do anything for her.

"Here you are, Mrs. Elliot." Filbert waved Mrs. Elliot into the library.

Amy stood and walked across the room to her. "Good evening, Mrs. Elliot. Can I assume you are all unpacked and settled in?"

"Yes, thank you so much, my lady. The room is very comfortable, and I must thank you once again for this opportunity."

Amy turned to introduce Mrs. Elliot. "May I present you to my aunt, Lady Margaret, Lord Wethington's parents, Lady Lily Colbert and Mr. Edward Colbert, and my father—"

Before she could continue, Papa set his drink down and walked forward. "I am Franklin, Lord Winchester." He reached for her hand which she extended, and he kissed the back of it. "And you are?"

Mrs. Elliot looked a tad flustered and glanced in Amy's direction.

"This is Mrs. Anne Elliot. We have hired her to take care of Mr. Mackay while he is recovering from the *ague*."

Just then Filbert returned to announce dinner. Papa took Mrs. Elliot's arm. "I will be happy to escort you, Mrs. Elliot."

Amy looked over at William with raised brows.

Aunt Margaret choked, trying to stop a laugh.

Lady Lily and Mr. Colbert grinned at each other.

Then they all followed a smiling Papa and Mrs. Elliot to the dining room.

11

_I_t was a lovely autumn day, but instead of walking to the vicarage, Amy had Benson take her there in the carriage because she had brought boxes with her to carry away whatever was left behind by Mr. Smythe.

William had intended to go with her to clear out the prior vicar's things but was called away before she left to deal with a problem one of the tenant farmers had. He'd told her it might take some time so she should go ahead without him.

She opened the vicarage door with the key Mrs. Peters had given her. As she unlocked the door, she realized either she or William should go to Mr. Graves and retrieve any items he found on Mr. Smythe's body.

The lack of response from the bishop about Mr. Smythe's family members was annoying, but after dealing with the Magistrate perhaps no one considered a murder in a small village important enough.

The vicarage was a small house, but well-kept and nicely furnished. There were two bedrooms, a dining area, an office, and a drawing room. It was a very comfortable home for a single man, but if the vicar came with a wife and family, things could get crowded.

Fortunately, someone—possibly Mr. Graves—had left a window open so the smell from the body was gone.

She opened the door to the vicar's office and gasped, her hands flying to cover her mouth. It wasn't that someone had left the window open. It had been smashed, and glass lay on the floor.

The desk was in disarray, and papers were strewn about. One of the drawers in the desk was open, and it appeared someone had rifled through it.

Could it be the person who murdered the vicar had returned to remove some evidence?

A bit rattled after her discovery, she decided the best way to get the job finished was to start with Mr. Smythe's personal belongings and clothing and then move back to the office and straighten things up. She hoped they would hear from the bishop soon about where to send Mr. Smythe's possessions.

She glanced out the window to make certain Benson was still sitting on top of the carriage. She knew it was silly, but it gave her a sense of security to have him there. Whoever broke into the vicarage could have been there only moments before.

Amy sighed when she walked into the vicar's bedroom. It was distressing to look upon items that he left scattered about, not knowing it would have been for the last time. Chastising herself for her maudlin thoughts, she pushed it all to the back of her mind. Determinedly, she began to collect things and placed them into the box.

The man did not own much. Two suits, vestments, shoes, a few shirts, and undergarments. She imagined Mr. Graves would have taken a timepiece and most likely the keys to the vicarage and the church from Mr. Smythe's body.

She opened the drawer in a small table under the window in the bedroom. She pulled out an appointment book and a bible. She added it to the other items and continued to survey the room.

Once everything from the bedroom was piled in the box, she moved into the office. She picked up all the papers from the floor, shuffling them together and placing them in another box. Once she got home, she would go through them, looking for clues. If she had, in fact, interrupted whoever had broken into the vicarage, he or she might not have found what they were looking for.

She placed the box of files and papers next to the one containing Mr. Smythe's clothing and personal belongings. With a thorough look around, it appeared everything that made the vicarage Mr. Smythe's home was gone. His entire life was contained in two cardboard boxes. She took a deep breath before she started crying.

Next, she would have to speak with Mrs. Peters and tell her she could clean and buy whatever food and supplies she would need for the new vicar to take possession of the vicarage.

She hurried from the house, telling Benson where he could find the two boxes, then handed him the key to lock up and decided to walk back to the Manor to clear her mind.

* * *

WILLIAM HAD RETURNED when she arrived at the Manor. The carriage was not in sight, so she assumed Benson had arrived and the boxes had been brought inside.

Lady Lily and Aunt Margaret were in the drawing room playing cards. Mr. Colbert was again nowhere in sight. She wondered how he spent his days since most days she didn't see him from after breakfast until dinner time.

"No, you should not be carrying that heavy tray." Papa's voice reached her from where he and Mrs. Elliot stood at the bottom of the stairs having a tug of war over a luncheon tray. She looked flustered; her papa determined.

"My lord, I am an employee. I was hired to take care of Mr. Mackay. One of my duties is to provide the man with his meals. I must do my job." She tugged back.

"Nonsense, you are doing your job. I just don't believe you should be doing the footmen's jobs." Papa tugged back again, but Mrs. Elliot was not loosening her grip.

Amy had to hide her giggle and decided it would be best if she intervened. She still had not gotten over Papa's reaction to Mrs. Elliot when he met her the night before at dinner. The only word that entered her mind all evening was 'smitten'. Something she would never, ever attribute to her papa.

"Mrs. Elliot, perhaps it would be best if you had a footman carry the heavier things upstairs for you."

Mrs. Elliot dipped her head, her face flushed.

"Since there are no footmen around, I shall carry it," Papa said, looking pleased, taking the tray fully into his hands as she finally released it.

They started up the stairs, and Amy joined William in the library where he sat behind his desk, bent over papers.

He looked up as she entered. "How was your trip to the vicarage?"

Amy dropped into the chair in front of his desk. "Aside from the fact that someone broke into the house, smashing a window and searching for who knows what, it went fine."

William's eyebrows rose as she spoke, and he leaned forward, placing his forearms on the desk. "Broke into the vicarage?"

"That would be correct. A window was shattered in the office, glass scattered all over. Whoever broke into the place riffled through the vicar's files in a drawer in the desk."

"And of course, there is no way of knowing who did it and why."

Amy shook her head. "I worried at one point that I had arrived shortly after the culprit left." She shivered. "However, Benson was right outside, and I could have called to him if there was a problem."

"I don't like the sound of that."

"All is well now. I will go through the papers I gathered and see if there are any clues there, but I'm sure whoever did it got what they were looking for."

"Maybe not," William said.

Amy nodded. "That is true." She stood and stretched. "I am ready for luncheon."

"I am, as well," William said. Just as he stood, Filbert entered the library to announce the meal was ready.

They were all seated when Papa returned from assisting Mrs. Elliot. They had just begun on their soup when Amy said, "Papa, you must understand that Mrs. Elliot is an employee. She will be quite uncomfortable if you insist on treating her like a guest."

Papa waved her off. "That woman should not be taking care of an invalid anyway. It is dirty work, and Mr. Mackay is quite demanding."

"Franklin, I understand your concern, but everyone who *works* here has to do dirty jobs now and again," William said, placing his spoon alongside his plate. At a nod to Carter, the footman assigned to luncheon picked up the dirty bowls and spoons.

He continued. "When we approached Mrs. Elliot about taking on this job, she was quite grateful. It seems she's had financial difficulties since her daughter married and was about to be removed from her house."

"Brother, you would be the first person to complain if any of your staff members asked for your assistance," Aunt Margaret added with a smirk.

"It is not right. No woman should be put from her house."

"Papa, that is why we asked Mrs. Elliot to stay here. She is quite comfortable in her room and is very appreciative of what we've done for her."

Papa said nothing further about it but grumbled to himself for a while about stubborn women.

"Well, family, I have an announcement to make," Mr. Colbert said with a smile as he wiped his mouth with his napkin and placed it back on his lap.

Apparently, Lady Lily was in on his secret because she took his hand and beamed.

"My lovely wife and I have purchased the bookstore in the village."

Amy's mouth dropped open. "What a surprise!" she said as they all began to speak at once.

Mr. Colbert held up his hand. "If you will give me a chance to explain, I can probably answer all your questions.

"When I first retired, I thought it would be wonderful. And it was. For about three days. I am not one who is accustomed to sleeping late in bed, wandering the house, and checking my timepiece numerous times a day. That's when we decided to come to the Manor and stay for a while to visit with family."

"And we are pleased to have you both," William said.

"You and Amy have been most gracious." He took a sip of water and continued as Carter placed platters of roasted chicken, boiled potatoes, and a compilation of various vegetables in the center of the table.

"When I visited Annabelle's Attic the day after our book club meeting, the lovely Mrs. Barnes and I had a conversation, and she mentioned she was thinking about selling the store and retiring to Brighton where she has a son and his family."

He looked at Lady Lily and smiled gently. "You all know I have a love for books, so it didn't take long for my wonderful wife to encourage me to buy the shop." He looked up at them all. "And we did!"

"How exciting, Edward," William said. "Mother, are you planning on having a hand in this?"

She beamed. "Of course. I have many plans to make the store a village gathering spot. I'm thinking of a tearoom where ladies can gather in the afternoon and discuss important matters that the men won't listen to us about."

Lady Margaret shook her head. "You are just full of surprises."

* * *

AFTER VISITING CHARLES, who was a tad cranky with getting new teeth, William and Amy settled in her solar to go through the boxes of items she had taken from the vicarage. For as undignified as it was, they decided to settle on the floor since it was easier than trying to balance the boxes on the settee.

"Has there been further news on the arrival of the new vicar?" Amy asked as she took the appointment book and bible from the box. The clothing would be donated to those in need.

"Nothing except the original missive about him arriving soon. Not even information on family members."

"I noticed in the bible that Mr. Smythe's name was written in there, but no other family members. Perhaps there is no one else to notify."

Amy flipped through the pages of the bible. "It seems sad to die and have no one to inform."

William took the bible from her hand. "I must write to the bishop again and once more ask about family members."

"We also must visit with Mr. Graves and retrieve any items he found on Mr. Smythe's body. I'm sure he had a timepiece and most likely the keys to the vicarage as well as the church and Fellowship Hall."

She picked up the appointment book and turned the pages. "Here is something interesting."

"What?" William placed the bible back into the box.

"He has Mr. Fletcher's name written down here a few times." She continued to turn the pages. "In fact, it looks as though he met with him once a week on Thursdays at two o'clock in the afternoon." She looked up at him. "Didn't Fletcher lose his wife last year?"

"Yes. Right after we moved into the Manor." William shrugged. "Most likely he was receiving grief counseling."

Amy climbed to her knees and pulled out the stack of papers and files she'd gathered from the floor of the vicarage. It took a while, but she managed to identify which papers went into each folder.

"There is no folder here for Mr. Fletcher. I would think if he was seeing the man on a regular basis that he would make some notes."

"Or," William said as he placed the stack of files back into the box, "they were just friends and maybe played chess or something like that once a week."

Amy stood and brushed her gown. "With the window in the vicarage being broken and files all scattered about but none for Mr. Fletcher, I think I will ask a few questions around town."

"You know it doesn't have to be something sinister. It's quite possible he and Mr. Smythe discussed things of a very personal nature that Fletcher just didn't want anyone to know about." William placed the two boxes on a table near the window.

"I believe we should put him on our suspect list, though," Amy said.

"You mean our very short suspect list? If memory serves, we only have Reynolds and an unknown woman who cried at the Inn with Mr. Smythe."

Amy tapped her lips with her fingertip. "You are absolutely correct. That should be our next step. Finding out who that woman is. We also need to speak with Mr. Davidson about that comment he made regarding Mr. Granger not being sad at Mr. Smythe's demise."

"So you see, dear wife, there are many things we should be doing if we want to solve this mystery."

Papa's voice bellowed from the bottom floor. "Mrs. Elliot, you should not be carrying that. It's much too heavy."

12

*T*hree days after Amy cleared out the vicarage, the new vicar arrived. She had not been able to visit in the village to gather more information since it turned out Charles had not been cranky due to a new tooth, but the lad had a cold with a slight fever and cough.

Of course, William had summoned a doctor immediately who advised the fretting parents to use a mustard plaster. However, he cautioned, it should not be on his skin for more than twenty or thirty minutes. He also suggested alternating the application between chest and back and using a cloth as a barrier between plaster and skin since it could be dangerous. He also advised keeping the windows closed and his little body swathed in linens.

After William told the doctor to leave before he threw him out the window, Mrs. Grover assured them that Charles was healthy, the cold mild, and there was no reason for concern. Despite her assurances, William had the footmen move the baby's crib from the nursery to their bedchamber. He and Amy took turns watching their son breathe and walking him up and down when he fussed.

Mrs. Grover enjoyed a few days off.

The new vicar, Mr. Stephen Hopkins, reached Wethingford quietly and settled into the vicarage, then sent a note to William that he had arrived. He didn't mention a wife or children, and since the bishop never sent any information except that he would arrive shortly, they had no way of knowing anything about the man.

"We must invite Mr. Hopkins for dinner," Amy said as she read the note that Mr. Hopkins had sent. Charles was back in the nursery, and as Mrs. Grover had said, it was a mild cold and he made a quick recovery. Unlike his parents who lost so much sleep there were dark circles under their eyes.

"Indeed. Tonight would be good since tomorrow being Sunday, he will most likely want to introduce himself to the congregation and give a short sermon. It will be good for us to welcome him and tell him a few things about the village and the people to whom he will be ministering."

Amy thought for a moment. "I notice he did not mention a wife."

"No, he doesn't, only that he has arrived and settled in. But it would be a good idea to tell Cook there might be more than one guest," William said.

"Very well, I shall speak with Cook and tell her we may have a guest for dinner and maybe two. Then we can have one of the footmen bring an invitation to the vicarage. I also think it would be good to ask Mrs. Peters to visit with some of the villagers and let them know that the new vicar has arrived. We don't want his first service to be sparsely attended."

"Do you have a minute, Amy?" Mr. Colbert asked as he entered the library.

She smiled at her father-in-law who looked and acted twenty years younger since he and Lady Lily had bought the bookstore. "Yes, of course. What do you need?"

"Are the villagers aware that you are the author E. D. Burton?"

"I believe some of them know. Those who visit the bookstore most likely. I never kept it a secret, and when I told Mrs. Barnes who I was, she made sure to always have my books on her shelves. Is there a reason you want to know this?"

Mr. Colbert nodded. "Yes. Mrs. Barnes has expressed a desire to leave as soon as possible now that she has decided to sell the bookstore. It appears the transition will take place next week. Lady Lily wishes to do some redecorating and put in her tearoom, which might involve some renovations as well. We shall be closed for a time—not long, I hope—and I was hoping once we are ready to re-open the bookstore that you would join us for a book signing."

Amy clasped her hands. "I would love to do that."

"Wonderful. I will keep you apprised of our progress." He left the room with a spring in his step that Amy had never seen before.

"This bookstore project has done wonders for your parents," Amy said.

She started for the library door. "With a few hours before dinner, I believe I will travel into the village and see if I can finally get some information on the crying woman and what Mr. Davidson meant when he said Mr. Granger would not be too sad to see Mr. Smythe gone."

"Excellent. I shall go with you."

They headed up to their bedchamber to prepare to leave. "I also need to speak with Mrs. Gabel about the Harvest Festival. I visited her last week, and she was going to ask some of the other women to help with getting the Festival organized."

William nodded as he changed into a fresh shirt. "I am sure Cook and Mrs. O'Sullivan will have excellent suggestions also. They were both here years ago when my parents held the Festival every year."

"A great suggestion, Husband. As housekeeper, Mrs. O'Sullivan would have a lot of information on the Festival." Amy paused. "And your mother. She would be a great help as well."

"Don't forget she is involved now in the bookstore. But I'm sure she can help with the Festival. At least with advice." He reached out and repositioned Amy's hat and fixed the button on her cape.

She hurried away before he could see that she was wearing two different shoes. The same shoes, actually, just different colors. But close. Dark blue and black.

With it being Saturday, all the vendors and pedlars were on the village green. "I hope it's not too difficult to speak with Lucy and Mr. Davidson," Amy said as the carriage came to a stop.

"We will do our best. It is after luncheon so the Inn might not be so busy. We should go there first. I could use one of their ales," William said as he took her arm, and they walked together hand in hand toward the Inn.

It appeared they might be in luck since there were only two other tables with patrons there. Lucy came to them right away. "Good afternoon, my lord, my lady. How are you today?"

"Well, thank you," William said. "I would like one of your ales." He looked over at Amy. "What would you like, my dear?"

"I think I will have an ale also."

Once Lucy set down their drinks, Amy said, "May I ask you something?"

"Of course," the girl said, glancing back at the kitchen. "I have a few minutes before I have to pick up some food."

"I was here almost two weeks ago with my sister-by-marriage for lunch. There was a young girl sitting at a table not far from us who was quite upset and crying. The vicar, Mr. Smythe, was sitting with her. Do you remember that?"

Lucy rested the tray she'd carried their drinks on against her hip. "Yes. That is a sad story." She paused. "I'd never seen her before that day. After Mr. Smythe left her, she sat there for a while and then called me over to ask for tea."

"Did she talk to you at all?"

"Yes. She was quite distraught. Her name is Miss Beatrice Harper, and she said she was engaged to the vicar."

"Mr. Smythe?" Amy said, her voice rising.

Lucy nodded. "That is what she said. They were engaged for a few months when he disappeared on her, and she tracked him here. She said he wasn't too happy to see her and told her he no longer wanted to marry her."

Amy looked over at William, them both wearing surprised expressions. "That is quite shocking," Amy said.

Lucy nodded. "Yes, I know. I was quite surprised myself. I didn't know the vicar was betrothed."

"I don't think anyone else did either," William added.

She nodded. "After a while, an older man joined her, and they left together."

"Have you spoken to her since then?"

Lucy turned as her father bellowed from the kitchen. "I must go. No, she never came in here again, but I did see her a few times when I was running errands."

"Well, that information was certainly not what I was expecting," Amy said as she and William left the Inn.

"It does cast a different light on the vicar, who everyone thought was perfect. To engage himself to a girl, then disappear," William said. "Not well done of him."

Amy took his arm as they made their way to the green. "I am assuming the older man who came to her at the Inn is the same one I saw her with when I was speaking with Mr. Davidson."

"Most likely. Did you want to go to the silversmith now and see if he can expand on his story about Mr. Granger's nonsadness at Mr. Smythe's passing?"

The sun that had been out earlier had disappeared while

they were enjoying their ales. William looked up at the gathering clouds. "I think we better make it a quick trip to Davidson's store. It's possible we might be drenched soon."

Just as he said that several of the vendors began glancing at the sky and gathering their wares to pack them away, apparently thinking the same thing. William and Amy hurried along through the throng and made it to the silversmith's just as the first raindrops fell.

"Good afternoon, my lord, my lady. It looks like you just made it in time." He gestured toward the window where the few raindrops had turned into rainfall. "What can I do for you? Are you interested in some fine pieces for the lady?" He looked at Amy. "Or perhaps you would like that fine piece you had your eye on for your husband?"

She laughed when William looked at her as if she was keeping something from him.

Not wanting to put him on edge by starting off questioning, Amy said, "May I see that inkwell again?"

"Certainly, my lady. I put it aside for you. Please excuse me for a minute while I retrieve it from my workshop."

"A silver inkwell?" William said.

Amy lowered her voice. "I needed something to talk about when I came in last week. I couldn't just walk up to the counter and say, 'Excuse me, Mr. Davidson, but do you know anything about Mr. Smythe's murder?'"

William smirked. "I have a feeling I will have a new silver inkwell sitting on my desk this afternoon."

"Here it is, my lord. Her ladyship chose this one but was unable to decide because she was distressed over the vicar's death."

Amy shook her head and allowed sadness to change her expression. "Yes. It was truly a sad incident." She looked up at Mr. Davidson. "If memory serves, I believe I mentioned how everyone was so distraught, but you thought one of your friends did not feel that way."

When Davidson didn't respond, William said, "I can't imagine anyone who was not upset by the vicar's death."

William and Amy both remained silent. The first one to speak lost. Mr. Davidson began to use a soft cloth to wipe fingerprints off the glass cases that displayed his jewelry. "Yes. I might have said something like that."

Amy snapped her fingers. "Yes, I remember now. I think you mentioned Mr. Granger."

The man took a deep sigh. "I probably should not have said that."

"But since you did, do you mind telling us why? We are curious since everyone did seem to hold the vicar in such high regard."

Mr. Davidson grunted and didn't meet their eyes. "Mr. Smythe was not what many think he was." He leaned in and looked back and forth as if the walls had ears. "He was dallying with Mr. Granger's wife."

Well, then.

"Indeed?" William said while Amy tried to digest this newest information about the beloved vicar.

Mr. Davidson raised his chin and sniffed. "Mr. Granger is a good friend. I have no reason to doubt his word." He picked up the inkwell. "If we may return to the matter at hand, do you wish to see this lovely piece gracing your desk, my lord?"

Realizing they weren't going to get any more information from the man, they left the shop, inkwell in hand, to find Benson had parked their carriage right in front of the store. The man deserved a raise.

It was a silent ride home while they digested the information they had received that afternoon.

"I guess we should add two more people to our list," William said.

Amy nodded. "Yes. We now have three. Mr. Reynolds, Mr. Fletcher, and Mr. Granger." She paused as the carriage hit a gouge in the road. "I think we should put the fiancée on our list as well."

She and William hurried up to their bedchamber to change their wet clothes for dinner. After checking with Mrs. Grover that Charles spent a quiet day chewing on his favorite toy, ate a hearty dinner, enjoyed his bath, and was now sound asleep for the night, William and Amy kissed the lad on the forehead and headed down to the drawing room for drinks before dinner.

They joined the Colberts and Aunt Margaret in the drawing room, enjoying a pre-dinner drink.

"Where is Papa?" Amy asked.

Aunt Margaret smiled. "He is attempting to persuade Mrs. Elliot to join us for dinner instead of eating with the staff."

"My goodness. I've never seen him so enthralled with a woman before," Amy said. She took a glass of sherry from William's hand. "We should probably straighten this out. Either decide to tell Mrs. Elliot she is welcome to join us, or tell Papa, as an employee, she must eat with the staff."

William shrugged. "I don't think Franklin will give up so easily."

Aunt Margaret placed her small glass on the table next to her. "When you were young, Amy, we had a governess for you. As a sort of in-between type of employee, she took her meals with us. Do you remember?"

"Yes. I do. Mrs. Campbell."

"When your sister was young, William," Lady Lily said, "her governess dined with the family as well."

William grinned. "I think you both have given me a way out. We shall declare Mrs. Elliot an in-between, temporary employee and advise her to join us for her meals."

Just then Papa and Mrs. Elliot entered the drawing room, Papa looking pleased and Mrs. Elliot looking resigned.

Filbert announced the arrival of Vicar Stephen Hopkins.

Amy and William moved toward the doorway as the new vicar entered. He was a pleasant looking man, somewhere in his forties or early fifties. His dark hair showed strands of silver. He wore spectacles, and his rotund figure presented a man who did not pass up many dinners.

"Mr. Hopkins, what a pleasure to meet you." William extended his hand. "I am Lord Wethington, and this is my wife, Lady Wethington."

Amy offered a warm smile. "I am so glad you are able to join us for dinner on such short notice, Mr. Hopkins."

"I am pleased to be here, Lady Wethington. Knowing no one in the village, I was most gratified to accept your invitation."

William waved in the direction of the sideboard. "Would you care for a drink before dinner?"

The vicar shook his head. "No. Thank you very much."

William finished the introductions of the other diners just as Filbert entered once more to announce dinner. They all headed to the dining room with Mr. Hopkins offering his arm to Lady Margaret, the only woman with no partner. Of course, Papa immediately extended his arm to Mrs. Elliot.

As they reached the dining room, Amy pulled William back.

He bent close to her face. "What is it?"

"I just remembered. We never asked Mr. Davidson about the young lady crying at the table with the vicar, then later showing up at the silversmith's with an older man."

"And?"

"That happened the day before Mr. Smythe's body was found."

13

"Where have you served before now?" Lady Margaret asked their guest.

Mr. Hopkins gave her a friendly but somewhat condescending smile. "Dear lady, I have served in so many places, it all comes together after a while." He wiped his mouth with his napkin. "However, my last assignment was in a small village in Scotland. I'm sure you've not heard of it. It's called North Berwick. Right there on the Firth of Forth. A lovely place."

"No, I don't believe I am familiar with Scotland," Lady Margaret said. "My husband is currently in Scotland, taking care of his uncle's estate," she added.

"Indeed? Where is he, my lady?"

"In the Highlands. I believe he said somewhere near Inverness."

"Ah, yes. Quite a distance from where I was."

The dinner continued with Mr. Hopkins peppering them with questions about the village and villagers. Aside from mentioning where he served last, he didn't have a lot to say about himself.

After they consumed the meal that Cook had outdone

herself with, they retired to the drawing room for tea and brandy, and again Mr. Hopkins passed on the brandy and took tea.

William sat back in his chair, crossing his legs. "Did you know Mr. Smythe?"

"Who?"

Surprised that he did not know the former vicar, he said, "Mr. Smythe is the vicar you are replacing."

"Ah, yes. The poor man who was murdered." He shook his head. "Sorry affair. I offered many prayers for his soul."

That created an awkward silence until the vicar placed his cup and saucer on the table in front of him. "I believe I shall be on my way. It grows late, and I have a service to conduct tomorrow." He looked around the room. "I can assume you will all be there to support me?"

"Of course," Lady Lily said.

The rest nodded their heads.

The vicar looked over at William. "May I indulge myself and ask to have your carriage return me to the vicarage? I walked here, but I'm afraid being new, and with the darkness, I may wander around for hours before I find my home." He let out a hearty laugh.

"Certainly," William said. "I will have Filbert send for the carriage."

While they waited for the vehicle, the talk turned to the weather and other innocuous subjects until Filbert announced the carriage was ready for the vicar.

They all stood with promises of attending church in the morning. Mr. Hopkins politely thanked William and Amy for a lovely dinner and left.

Once the door closed, they sat back down. William headed to the sideboard for another brandy. He turned to the group and held up the decanter.

"Yes. I will join you," Edward said.

Franklin shook his head, which was a surprise to William because he rarely refused a drink.

William took his seat, swirling the brown liquid in his glass. "What is the general consensus about Mr. Hopkins?"

"It is really hard to say," Aunt Margaret said. "He is not as charming as Mr. Smythe, but I don't believe being charming is a requirement to serve."

"No, indeed," Lady Lily said. She took her last sip of tea. "But then, even though I've been here for a short time, I believe it would have been difficult to replace Mr. Smythe. Everyone loved him."

Amy looked over at William. "Not everyone, it seems."

That brought another stretch of silence as they all remembered the man had been murdered.

Mrs. Elliot, who had been quiet most of the night, stood. William, Franklin, and Edward climbed to their feet.

"Oh, you mustn't stand. I am going to check on Mr. Mackay and then retire." She looked at Amy. "Thank you so much for inviting me this evening, my lady. It was a pleasure to meet the new vicar. I think he will do well here."

Franklin moved forward. "I will see to Mackay with you."

If Mrs. Elliot was surprised or annoyed, she did not show it, but allowed Franklin to lead her to the staircase.

Lady Margaret stared after them. "I believe someone kidnapped my brother and sent this lookalike here in his place."

* * *

"I AM FRUSTRATED, Husband. We are no closer to solving Mr. Smythe's murder than we were the day after the body was discovered." Amy finished dressing for church and studied herself carefully to make sure everything was as it should be.

William shrugged into his jacket and motioned for her to leave the room. "At least we have a few people on our list now."

"Yes. But very little to point to any of them."

"If you had to put one person at the top of the list, who would it be?" William asked as they stepped off the staircase onto the entrance hall floor and he handed her forgotten reticule to her.

She sighed and took it from his hands.

The discussion ended there when the others joined them for the trip to church. Both William's carriage and Papa's carriage sat in front of the Manor. William, Amy, and the Colberts climbed into the Wethington carriage while Aunt Margaret, Franklin, and Mrs. Elliot claimed the Winchester vehicle.

"Have you had a chance to speak with Mrs. Elliot yet about taking her meals with us?" William asked.

"Yes. I saw her this morning when we left the breakfast room. At first, she tried to dissuade me, but then she accepted that her role was an in-between one since this was temporary employment and she was not an official member of the staff."

"We will have to find something suitable for her once Mr. Mackay recovers," William said.

He shifted in his seat as the carriage moved forward. "That reminds me. Has anyone except Mrs. Elliot seen this man recovering in our home? I mean, he's been here for some time now and shouldn't he be on his way soon?"

"I think this afternoon I shall visit him and see what the progress is," Amy said.

Lady Lily smiled at them. "I have a feeling Mr. Mackay has no intention of ever 'recovering.'"

"I'm sure he has a home, and I know he has a job to return to. I'm surprised the Magistrate has not written to check on his employee's welfare. After I received the missive from Sir Archibald that Mr. Mackay should remain and conduct the investigation, I replied with the information that the man was ill," William added.

"Do you believe the Magistrate is anxious for Mr. Mackay to return?" Amy asked. "I don't believe he performs such a service to the office that he is severely missed. In fact, I believe Sir Archibald sending him here was to get Mr. Mackay away from him."

They arrived at the church, and apparently word had spread that the new vicar had arrived and was giving his first sermon this morning. Carriages and horses were haphazardly parked in the area both alongside and behind the building.

Even though the vicar had only just arrived a day or so before, the ladies had managed to arrange a meal to follow the service in the Fellowship Hall. Not being aware of it, Amy watched with guilt as woman after woman walked to the hall carrying bowls and platters of food and desserts.

"I should have baked something for the luncheon today," she said as she watched the parade of food.

"No!" Lady Lily and Aunt Margaret said together.

Lady Lily smiled at her and patted her hand. "No need to feel guilty, dear. As you can see, there is plenty of food."

Amy never understood why they were all so adamant about her not baking anymore. She thought she'd done some very tasty recipes. At least that was what William had said. Many times, however, he was much too full from dinner to enjoy them.

They entered the church. The first two pews, as was expected, were empty, being held for the Lord and Lady and their family. Once they settled in the pews, more congregants entered the church and took seats.

The organist began playing. Amy sometimes missed Mrs. Edith Newton, the organist from St. Swithin's church that Amy had attended all her life before moving to the Manor. The sweet lady always played off-key, but everyone loved her and sang along—off-key—rather than hurt her feelings.

After a few minutes of music to allow everyone to settle in their seats, William rose, turned, and addressed the congregation. "It is my pleasure this morning to introduce to you, Mr. Stephen Hopkins, our new vicar."

A slight applause followed; the congregants apparently not sure if that was appropriate in church.

Mr. Hopkins came out of the side door of the sanctuary and took his place at the front of the church. "Good morning."

He continued for about thirty minutes with an, unfortunately, rather insipid sermon. Certainly nothing like the ones Mr. Smythe offered, although it didn't seem very Christian-like to compare the two men.

After a few more hymns and an announcement about luncheon in the Fellowship Hall, they all left the church.

Papa, of course, escorted Mrs. Elliot, who appeared a tad uncomfortable as others in the parish regarded her with curiosity. She had been well-known as the village seamstress, and now she was on the arm of a member of the nobility.

Aunt Margaret walked up to Amy and linked her arm in hers. "Do you think Franklin is serious about Mrs. Elliot?"

Amy studied him. "I have no idea. You know him better and longer than I do. As you know, I only saw him a few times a year when he visited us in Bath. Then there was that disastrous Season in London where we were at odds all the time since I wanted to return home to Bath, and he was insistent I would marry a titled gentleman."

Aunt Margaret tugged her close. "And you did marry a lord with a title. Without Franklin's help and with a man who adores you."

Amy huffed. "I doubt William adores me. I think it's more like he feels compelled to direct my life to keep me safe and out of trouble."

Her aunt shook her head. "Do not fool yourself, Niece."

They reached the Fellowship Hall which was a bevy of activity. Amy noticed the vicar was speaking with several people, then moved along to speak to more. He seemed like a friendly man, and hopefully his sermons would get better.

Mr. Granger sat at one of the long tables next to them. His wife was with him, and Amy noticed they didn't speak much to each other, or to anyone else for that matter. It was apparent there was some strain between them.

Mr. Hopkins cleared his throat, and everyone in the room grew silent. He made a short speech, did not bless the food, and walked to the table with scores of bowls and platters on it to fill his plate. Since that appeared to be a signal for the rest of them, a line formed as each congregant began to select items from the offerings.

"Lady Amy, may I have a minute?" Mrs. Gabel approached their table.

Since he was finished eating, William stood. "Here, Mrs. Gabel, take my seat. I am about to take a stroll around the room anyway."

"Oh, thank you, my lord. You are most kind."

Once the woman was settled in the seat, she turned to Amy. "I was wondering if you could spare an afternoon or perhaps an evening to meet with the committee ladies we've put together for the Harvest Festival?"

"Of course. Afternoons would be better for me, but if that's not possible, I can do an evening."

"Oh, no, my lady. We are honored that you would join is. Would Thursday afternoon be too soon?"

Amy thought on the upcoming week. "Yes. Thursday would be fine."

"Thank you so much, my lady." The woman seemed relieved.

"Would you all come to the Manor? I'm sure my aunt and

mother-in-law would like to be involved. We shall have a tea party."

Mrs. Gabel looked as though she would cry. "Thank you so much. I can't tell you how happy we all are that you and Lord Wethington have decided to make this your home. We so loved having the family here when his lordship and his sister were growing up."

Amy patted her hand. "And we are happy to be here, as well. We think this is a wonderful place to raise our son."

Blotting her eyes, Mrs. Gabel excused herself and left, hurrying over to a few women who apparently were waiting for her return.

"Whatever did you say to Mrs. Gabel?" William asked. "She is wiping her eyes."

Amy shrugged. "Nothing. I just offered to have a meeting she wanted to have about the Harvest Festival at the Manor."

William wandered off, and Amy ate the last of the lovely apple tart sitting on her plate, promising herself she would most assuredly remove sweets from her menu tomorrow.

She had just finished and felt the ensuing guilt when Lady Lily leaned across Aunt Margaret. "Are we ready to depart? Edward and I would like to spend some time going over our plans for the bookstore."

"Yes, I believe so." Amy stood and walked to where William spoke with Mr. Fletcher. The man looked uncomfortable.

"Your parents would like to leave, William. They have plans for the afternoon."

William held out his hand and Mr. Fletcher took it, and they shook.

"I am ready, my love. Let us head for the carriage. That is, if we can find it with that jumble of horses and carriages outside."

It turned out that Papa and Mrs. Elliot and Aunt Margaret were all ready to leave, too, so they were fortunate enough to find their carriages next to each other. It took some maneuvering, but Benson was able to get the carriage free of the others and they headed home.

"I'm going up to spend time with Charles," Amy said as she removed her hat and cape and handed them to Filbert.

William removed his coat, hat, and gloves, and handed them off also. "I will join you."

Charles was in a fine mood. He had recovered from his cold and apparently whatever tooth had been bothering him had fully erupted.

William stretched out on the floor and teased the baby with his timepiece again. Once Charles grew frustrated with not being able to grab it, he began to cry. Amy picked him up and placed him on her lap. "Here, my little love, a soft animal is just the thing." She handed him one of his soft toys which he immediately put in his mouth.

The door to the nursery opened, and to Amy's shock, Aunt Margaret walked in. "I thought I would visit with Charles for a little bit."

"Of course," Amy said, looking over at William.

Aunt Margaret smirked. "Don't look so shocked, Niece. I am going to have to deal with this in a few months."

Amy decided not to remind Aunt Margaret that she planned to have nurses, nannies, and governesses for her child.

She took the baby from Amy's arms and sat on one of the comfortable chairs in the nursery. For a minute, she looked like she didn't know what to do with the lad.

Then she jiggled the baby on her knee, smiling at him. He giggled and laughed back at her.

Right before he brought up his last meal onto her lap.

14

The next afternoon, William and Amy arrived at the bedroom where Mr. Mackay was supposedly recovering from his *ague*.

After a soft knock, Mrs. Elliot opened the door and smiled at them.

"We would like to speak with Mr. Mackay," Amy said.

She opened the door wider, and they stepped inside.

"You may take a break, Mrs. Elliot," William said.

She dipped and left the room as Amy and William approached the bed. Mr. Mackay lay on the mattress, numerous soft pillows propping him up. He was the picture of health. He looked even better than when he'd arrived.

"How are you feeling, Mr. Mackay?" Amy asked.

He sighed. "No' good, lass. 'Tis a bad thing to catch the *ague* when ye are an old mon." For emphasis, he amused them with a fake cough.

William looked around the room, his eyes landing on the lunch tray. It appeared the man had been served some sort of beef. That was obvious because smears of gravy from the meat were the only thing left on the plate. He apparently had a glass of milk, which was empty, and some sort of dessert, the stickiness evident on the small plate.

Like it or not, the man was still their guest. "Are you comfortable?" he asked.

"Aye. That is, as comfortable as a mon can be when he's sick." Another fake cough.

William looked over at Amy as she tried to hide her grin.

"And is Mrs. Elliot treating you well?" Amy asked.

"Aye, lass. Looking at her makes my illness bearable." Cough, cough.

William took Amy's hand. "I am glad to hear all is well. I hope you have a speedy recovery."

Mr. Mackay inhaled deeply and shook his head, closing his eyes. "'Tis no' easy when ye are older, lad."

They left the room, holding in their laughter until they reached their bedchamber. Amy wiped her eyes. "That is the healthiest old man I've ever seen in my life."

"Did you notice his lunch tray?" William asked.

"No. I was too busy trying to pretend I sympathized with him. What was on the tray?"

"Empty dishes." William grinned. "The man has quite an appetite for an old, sickly man."

"I fear your mother is correct, and Mr. Mackay will be with us for a while."

William sat on the edge of the bed. "Since Charles has just gone down for his nap, I suggest we visit the village again and ask enough questions to get this solved."

"I agree. I just need to meet with Mrs. O'Sullivan for a brief time." Amy headed toward the door. "I will be able to leave in less than a half hour."

William headed to the door. "I shall be in the library, trying to find something, anything, to move this along."

Once they arrived in the village, they decided to stop at the bookstore since his parents had set off for the store right after luncheon. The door to the store was open, and his mother swept the floor.

His mother.

Swept the floor.

His mother, who he doubted had ever held a broom in her hands in her life, swept the floor.

They stepped out of the carriage and gave instructions to Benson, then entered the building. "Mother, I cannot believe you are sweeping the floor."

She beamed. "Isn't it wonderful? Edward insisted that the bookstore be in both of our names. This is the first time in my life I own something and can take care of it. By myself. No staff to attend me."

"Mother, I can send one of our maids to do this for you."

Edward walked up behind her and placed his arm around her shoulders. "I told your mother we should hire someone, but she insisted this was her project."

His mother never ceased to amaze him. She had been a widow for fifteen or so years when she moved in with him a couple of years ago, joined the book club that he and Amy had belonged to, and met Mr. Edward Colbert.

For as immediately smitten as Franklin appeared to be with Mrs. Elliot, the same could be said for the very brief courtship of Colbert and his mother. They both seemed happy, and that was enough for him.

"Excuse my interruption, but may I speak with the owner, please?" A young woman had entered the store while they were talking.

For some reason, Amy stepped up to her. "How can I help you?"

"I'm looking for a job, and I understand this bookstore was just bought from Mrs. Barnes."

Amy took the girl's elbow and walked her over to the

counter in the front of the store. She pointed to one of two chairs. "Please, have a seat. I will be right with you."

She hurried over to where William, Edward, and Mother stood, staring at her. Amy pulled Mother aside. "My apologies for stepping in like this, but I have been wanting to speak with this young lady for days."

William leaned down, close to Amy's ear. "Is this the girl crying at the Inn?"

"Yes," Amy said. "This is a great opportunity to get information from her." She looked at his mother. "Are you planning to hire staff?"

Mother and Edward looked at each other. "I don't think we've thought that far ahead."

"That is fine," Amy said. "I will not promise her a job but will tell her to return in a week or so. Is that acceptable?"

"Yes," Mother said. She looked over at the young woman. "She seems like a nice person."

William studied the girl for a minute. "I shall go with you, but I'll let you speak with her."

William and Amy walked over to the counter. Amy sat down next to her, and William stood behind them, leaning his shoulder on the window frame, his arms crossed.

Amy pulled out a piece of paper from under the counter. "I am Lady Wethington and behind me is my husband, Lord Wethington."

Her eyes grew wide. "Oh, dear. You are the ones the village is named for. I don't believe you would be interested in hiring me." She made to stand, but Amy placed her hand on hers. "Please, don't leave." She looked over at his mother and Edward as they were busy taking books off shelves and placing them on a table.

"We don't own the store. Lord Wethington's parents do, and we are helping them out."

The woman looked leery, but she settled back in the chair.

Pencil poised over the paper, Amy asked, "What is your name?"

"Miss Beatrice Harper." She watched as Amy wrote the information down.

Amy looked up at her. "I admit I am not familiar with everyone in the village, but I don't believe I know you. Have you lived here long?"

She shook her head. "No. I've only been here for a week or two."

Amy nodded and wrote on the paper, then looked up at the woman with a warm smile. "And what brings you to our little village?"

Miss Harper raised her chin. "To meet with my fiancé."

So far what she said was the same information Amy had gotten from Lucy. "And did you see him?"

"Yes. But we are no longer engaged. Can you tell me if there is an opportunity for a job?"

This was a subject that young Miss Harper did not want to discuss. William could certainly understand that. He hoped Amy wouldn't pursue it.

"I can tell you that Lady Lily, who owns the store with her husband Mr. Colbert, have just taken it over and I know she probably has a lot of work to do. Can you tell me where you are staying? Have you taken a permanent home?"

Miss Harper nodded. "Yes. A friend came with me and helped me find a place to live."

Amy tapped her lips with the pencil. "I don't want to be intrusive, Miss Harper, but if you came here to meet your fiancé and are no longer engaged, why did you decide to stay?"

Her eyes filled with tears, and she took a deep breath. "Because I have nowhere else to go." She stood, clutching her reticule. "If you will excuse me, my lady, I will continue my job search."

"Wait," Amy said. "Before you go, write down your direction

so we can contact you if Lady Lily and Mr. Colbert decide they need to hire someone. Or you might try returning in a few days once they are more settled."

Miss Harper took Amy's pencil and scribbled on the bottom of the paper. She gave them both a quick curtsey and left the store.

William took the young girl's seat. "I'm assuming the friend she had with her is the one who found her a place to stay."

"Yes. I'm thinking that her and her friend's trip to Mr. Davidson's shop was to sell something."

He nodded. "Perhaps a betrothal ring."

"It is interesting that she said she had nowhere to go. I'm assuming that meant no family to provide for her."

"I think another trip to Mr. Davidson's store is in order," William said. "I'd like to know if it was a betrothal ring she was intending to sell and if he learned anything after speaking with her and her friend."

* * *

AMY FOLDED the paper she'd been writing Miss Harper's information on, then stood and followed William over to where the Colberts were stacking books.

"We took the young lady's information. She gave us her direction so we can seek her out if you decide you need an employee. I also told her to check back with you," Amy said as she tucked the paper with the information into her reticule.

"Thank you, dear. I am sure we will need at least one and most likely more to run the store. Neither one of us wants to spend all our time here."

William leaned over and kissed his mother on the cheek. "Don't forget to finish your sweeping."

"I also wanted to ask if you were interested in helping with the Harvest Festival," Amy said.

Lady Lily gasped. "The Harvest Festival! That's wonderful. I didn't know you were thinking about having it again. I had so much fun doing it when we lived here years ago. Once your father died and I moved to London, I forgot all about it."

William nodded. "I remember it from when I was a boy. Mrs. Gabel approached me about it when I visited her and her husband a while back. She was so very excited when I told her it would be our honor to hold it again."

"Mrs. Gabel approached me at the luncheon after church on Sunday and said she and some of the ladies wanted to have a meeting this week to go over some things. They, apparently, have been doing planning themselves already," Amy said.

"That sounds wonderful. When is the meeting?"

"Thursday afternoon. I told Mrs. Gabel I would be happy to hold the meeting at the Manor and provide tea and we could have a tea party."

Lady Lily looked up at her husband. "You will have to do without me Thursday afternoon, dear. I think having the Harvest Festival again will certainly bring happiness to the community, which we can use after the tragedy."

He patted her hand. "Whatever you want, my love. I can certainly handle things here for one afternoon. We are not even open yet, so I'll just be arranging things."

"But not my tearoom." She wagged her finger. "I want to do that. She turned to Amy. "It turns out we can enjoy a tearoom without having to add onto the store. Edward was wonderful in figuring out how to do it." She beamed at her husband as if he hung the moon.

William took Amy's arm. "We must be off. It is growing close to the time to return home and prepare for dinner, and we have one more stop to make."

Lady Lily and Mr. Colbert waved them off, and they headed across the green to the silversmith's shop. The store was empty except for Mr. Davidson who worked on a piece of jewelry.

He turned when they entered. "Good afternoon, my lord, my lady. Are you here for another fine piece of silver? Perhaps a cup to place on your desk to hold pen nibs?"

William realized it would be easier to speak with the man if he thought he was about to make a sale. "I am pleased with the inkwell, and it looks grand on my desk. However, before we delve into that, my wife and I would like some information from you."

"What is that my lord?"

Amy smiled at him. "Did you know that his lordship's parents, Lady Lily and Mr. Colbert, have purchased Mrs. Barnes' bookstore?"

He shook his head. "No. I did not know that. I didn't realize the good woman was interested in selling it. She's been there for years."

"Yes, she has. But she wanted to retire and move closer to her son and his family."

He began to wipe the glass counter with a soft cloth. "Yes, I know she was getting up there in years. I am happy for her."

"We just now left the store, and while we were there, a young lady came in looking for a job."

He studied her, his brows furrowed. "Yes?"

"She gave us her name as Miss Beatrice Harper. I am quite sure she is the young lady who was in here with an older man a week or so ago when I stopped in and looked at the silver inkwell for his lordship."

Mr. Davidson stopped rubbing the glass and stared off for a minute. "Yes. I do believe I remember her. She was here to sell a ring."

Amy and William glanced at each other. "The point of us asking is she is new to the village, and we wanted to secure more information about her before Lady Lily considers employing her."

That sounded like a weak excuse to Amy, but Mr. Davidson

didn't appear to think it odd. He nodded. "She was a lovely young lady. It was hard for me to tell her the ring was not worth much. A fake stone, you see."

"If you were seeking to hire someone, did Miss Harper give you any reason to not employ her?"

"No. She was unhappy about the ring, of course, and disappointed with how much I could offer her for it, but she was pleasant about it. The older gentleman who was with her apparently was someone she had met on the train and offered to escort her from the railway station to Wethingford."

"That was very nice of him," Amy said.

"Yes. He offered to stay for a while to see her settled, but she thanked him and told him that was not necessary."

William shook Mr. Davidson's hand. "Thank you, then, for your observations of Miss Harper. My mother will be happy to know that if she decides to hire her."

They left the store and headed back to where the carriage had been parked. "Things are beginning to look worse for Mr. Smythe all the time," Amy said. "A fake ring, a fake betrothal." She shook her head. "The poor girl."

"Yes. It appears not *everyone* did have a reason to love him."

They both looked up at the sound of shouting coming from in front of the Inn. Mr. Reynolds and his son-in-law, Joseph Hamilton, were nose-to-nose, Reynolds waving his hands in the air.

William turned them to walk in that direction. "Here now, what is all the shouting about?"

Joseph stepped away just as Reynolds took a swing at him.

William moved behind the man and pulled him back. "Calm down, Reynolds."

Amy walked over to Joseph. "What is this all about?"

Joseph backed up and glared at Reynolds. "He says he intends to speak with the new vicar about having my marriage to Jane annulled because we didn't have his permission."

William looked at Reynolds. "I thought that was all settled. Vicar Smythe stated that since Jane was over the age of consent, they didn't need your permission."

Reynolds yanked himself away from William. "Well, we will see about that. Maybe this new vicar will see things differently."

William nodded at Joseph. "Go on home, lad. Pay no attention to Mr. Reynolds."

Joseph stormed off, turning back to shout at Reynolds as he made his way across the green, heading in the direction of his farm.

"Reynolds, give up on this. The young people are married and happy."

The man raised his fist and shook it. "Not if I have my way."

*a*my viewed the array of small sandwiches and sweets Cook had prepared for her tea with the ladies who were working on the Harvest Festival. "This looks lovely, Mrs. Randolph. You always do such a wonderful job."

The cook beamed. "Oh, my lady, it is so easy to please you. I must admit we were all a tad worried when you married his lordship and then moved from your home in Bath to the Manor. We had heard stories of new wives coming into a home and wreaking havoc with the staff."

"Ah, I am so happy that you are pleased with me." She took a biscuit off the tray and bit into it. "Perfect, as always. When my guests arrive, please have one of the footmen bring the tea things to my solar."

After informing Filbert that she was expecting several ladies and he should direct them to her solar, she headed upstairs to where the meeting would be held. As she reached the corridor, Mrs. Elliot approached her.

"My lady, Mr. Mackay is napping right now. Would it be acceptable for me to attend your meeting? I always worked on the Harvest Festival years ago. It was so much fun, even though a lot of work. I can't tell you how happy I am that you and his lordship have agreed to have it once more."

"Of course, Mrs. Elliot. We would love to have you join us. The more help we have, the easier the load for everyone."

They strolled together to Amy's solar. Once they were seated, Amy asked, "How is Mr. Mackay faring? Does his health seem improved?"

Mrs. Elliot smiled. "I hate to tell you this, my lady, since Mr. Mackay is here at your largess, and once he recovers, I will be unemployed, but the man is quite well. He is enjoying his stay here, and I believe he has no interest in returning to his prior life."

"Really? Doesn't he have a family or a home he wishes to return to?"

The woman shook her head. "We talk a lot while I am attending him. He is alone in the world. He is fully aware that his job will end soon since the Magistrate has told him so."

"Oh, dear. The poor man." This certainly created a problem for them. How could they send an old man off to his home when there was no one to support him?

She patted Mrs. Elliot's hand. "Do not fret about your job. His lordship will find something for you. And I doubt my papa would be happy to see you leave."

Mrs. Elliot's face turned red at the mention of her father.

Amy had spent the past two days catching up on her writing. Aside from visiting Charles, she remained in her office, even asking for trays to be sent up for her meals. She was in the middle of her current murder mystery and had put it aside to concentrate on a real murder.

Again.

Finally, William had arrived at her office last evening, picked her up, and carried her to their bedchamber, dropping her on the bed in a very ignominious manner. "Enough, my dear author. You need some rest, and your eyes, and my ears, need a break from that infernal typing machine."

Filbert entered the room with four ladies behind him, interrupting her ruminations. "My lady, Mrs. Gabel, Mrs. Waters, Miss Martin, and Mrs. Applegate have arrived."

The four ladies offered greetings to Amy and Mrs. Elliot, all acting as though months had passed since they last saw them, even though Amy had seen Mrs. Applegate and Miss Martin at the book club meeting the week before. Last night should have been their meeting, but Lady Lily and Edward were refashioning the bookstore, so the book club meetings had been paused until the new shop opened.

They had no sooner settled themselves when Lady Lily and Aunt Margaret followed them in.

"I decided to join you. It will give me something to keep me occupied," Aunt Margaret said. "I find of late I cannot concentrate on anything. I tried sketching and painting, but it looks awful, and I lose interest."

Lady Lily air kissed the other women, all of them remarking on how excited they were to once again have the Festival.

"You are looking well, Lady Margaret. When is your babe due?" Mrs. Applegate asked.

Her aunt shrugged. "Sometime in March." She shifted in her seat. Even though she was now into her fourth month, she had expanded quite a bit. Hopefully, she wouldn't pull a surprise as Eloise had by giving birth to twins.

Poor Aunt Margaret was not taking this whole thing very well. Of course, she was sure Charles emptying his stomach all over her hadn't helped either.

"Goodness, you aren't married very long, are you?" Mrs. Applegate asked.

What was the woman doing, counting months?

Aunt Margaret raised her chin. "We married last March."

Amy could see Mrs. Applegate counting in her head. "It's quite interesting that someone of your age became with child so soon."

Aunt Margaret looked as though she was tempted to yank the dark blue bird perched on top of Mrs. Applegate's hat and stuff it down her throat. Instead, she smiled. "I am just a female wonder."

Mrs. Applegate merely sniffed.

Carter pushed the tea tray into the room, the ladies all exclaiming over the treats presented.

Amy and Lady Lily poured the tea and passed it around. Aunt Margaret placed tidbits on small plates and handed them out to the ladies. It was all done in a very systematic manner which gave Amy hope they could all work together harmoniously.

That hope was quickly smothered after a half hour of everyone speaking over everyone else. The women who had been in the village for years wanted everything to be the same. Amy and Aunt Margaret wanted new and fresh.

Lady Lily whispered to Amy that she was torn between her old friends and her family, while Amy considered returning to her office and continuing her story.

Eventually, voices softened, and Lady Lily stood and addressed the group. "Ladies, I understand that those of us who remember the wonderful Harvest Festivals from years ago struggle with change, but my daughter-in-law and Lady Margaret have good points also. Perhaps we can combine the event. Keep some of the old favorites and add some new events."

William arrived at the doorway. "Good afternoon, ladies. Am I to assume this is the committee for the Harvest Festival?"

"Yes. We are discussing what events to hold and which ones to do away with so we can add the new ones," Lady Lily said.

Just then several of the women began to speak over each

other again. William walked to the tea tray, picked up two small sandwiches and a tart, and left the room.

"Coward," Amy called after him, although with the racket, she was certain he hadn't heard her.

* * *

"I'M NOT sure we should keep Miss Harper on our suspect list," William said the next day as he and Amy set out once again for the village.

"Why not?"

William shrugged. "Remember, the vicar was shot in the chest. Do you honestly believe now that you've met her that Miss Harper could aim a gun at her fiancé and shoot him?"

"I don't think we should remove her just yet. We've only spent about ten minutes with the young lady and, yes, she seems quiet and vulnerable, but that doesn't mean she could not kill him." She smirked at William. "I believe you were taken by her soft demeanor, and the protectiveness of your nature refuses to believe she could kill someone. Let's see how our meeting with Mr. Granger goes before we remove anyone from the list."

They had arranged to meet with Mr. Granger at the Inn for luncheon. Since the man owned the Sundry Shop, Amy had suggested they visit him on the pretense of asking for a donation of a few small toys and candy sticks to give to the children of the villagers who come to the Festival. The man would certainly benefit from the event since the ladies were all buying supplies for baking pies and cakes and using yarn from his shop to finish up blankets and other items to display and enter various competitions.

They found Mr. Granger sitting at a table near the back of the Inn, sipping on a mug of ale. He rose as they joined him. "Good day, my lord, my lady."

After greeting him in return, they sat, and Lucy was right there with two mugs of ale for her and William.

"How are you, Lucy?" Amy asked as the girl set the mugs down.

She bobbed. "Just fine, my lady. And you are well also?"

She might have said she was fine, but Amy noticed she appeared quite fatigued. Apparently, her father continued to work the girl much too hard.

"Yes, I am quite well." Amy took a sip of her ale. "What is your special today?"

"Fish stew. It's very good, if I might say so myself."

"I will have that," Mr. Granger said.

She and William agreed, and Lucy hurried away.

"Are you aware that the villagers are planning a Harvest Festival in a couple of weeks?" William asked.

Granger frowned. "No. I thought they had done away with that."

"When I was living in Bath and my mother in London, we didn't hold them, and apparently whatever vicars were here during that time didn't make an effort to continue the tradition. However, the ladies have decided it is time to enjoy the feast again."

"Mr. Granger," Amy said, "I am working with a group of ladies to organize the event. Do you think your wife would be interested in helping us?"

His face lost all expression, and he downed the rest of his ale. Before he could answer her question, Lucy arrived with a tray of three bowls of fish stew, a loaf of warm bread, and a crock of butter.

It appeared Mr. Granger used the delivery of their food to ignore her question. They ate in silence with occasional comments on the tastiness of the dish.

Eventually, Mr. Granger wiped his mouth with his napkin and placed it alongside his plate. "My wife is currently visiting her mother. I don't expect her to return for a while."

Amy glanced at William. If what Mr. Davidson had said was true, then once Mr. Smythe died, it might have caused the Granger marriage to suffer. Did Mrs. Granger suspect her husband killed the vicar out of jealousy? Is that why she fled to her mother? Or was it simply grief for the death of her lover?

William pushed away his empty bowl. "We are asking the various shop owners to participate in the Festival by becoming involved."

Granger's eyes narrowed. "Involved how? I have a business to run."

"Nothing like that, Mr. Granger," Amy said. "We hoped you might donate some small toys or candy sticks to give out to the children who attend with their parents."

He nodded. "I can do that." He took a glance at his time-piece. "I must return to my store. I don't like leaving it closed more than a half hour for lunch."

"Don't you have an employee to help out?" Amy remembered the store as always being quite busy.

"My *employee* is off visiting her mother."

She wracked her brain for a way to bring up the vicar's death. Finally, she placed her hands in her lap and looked at Mr. Granger. "The Festival is a bit late this year. We have set a date of the fourteenth of October to have our celebration."

She sighed. "We didn't want to have it sooner due to Mr. Smythe being killed in his own home. It has certainly cast a shadow over the town, setting most of the villagers on edge. The man was so loved."

Granger's face grew red, and he hopped up from his chair, anger radiating from every part of his body. "I do not wish to discuss the vicar." He tossed a couple of coins on the table and strode from the Inn, opening the door so hard it slammed against the wall.

"Oh, my," Lucy said as she stared at Granger stomping down the steps. "What was that all about?"

William studied the man as he almost knocked a woman over in his hurry to get to his store. "That is a good question, Lucy. A very good question."

"Things are becoming so different in the village lately," Lucy said as she picked up their dirty dishes."

"How so?" William asked.

"Well, Mr. Smythe was murdered." She shuddered. "Then Mr. Reynolds seems to fight with everyone. Just last night he was in here, drunk again, and was spouting off about the new vicar. Said some mean things about him." She shook her head and wiped the table with a cloth. "Joseph Hamilton and his new wife, Jane, stopped in two days ago and said Mr. Reynolds was still trying to claim their marriage would be annulled. He said it was a good thing he had a gun because if Reynolds came after Jane, he would shoot him."

16

"I wonder if either Miss Harper or Mr. Granger own a gun, too?" Amy asked as they left the Inn after Mr. Granger's outburst and Lucy's revelations.

"That is a good question. Also, although we hadn't put Joseph on our list of suspects, if he thought Mr. Smythe would grant the annulment, he might have killed him."

"That seems terribly weak, William. Mr. Reynolds had no case in that matter, and he had to know that. To my way of thinking, it would make more sense in that situation for Reynolds to kill Joseph, making Jane a widow."

"That's an uncomfortable thought. However right now I suggest we stop in to see Mr. Morris over at the Forge." William took her arm, and they made their way across the green to the Smithy.

To their surprise, Miss Harper was leaving the place as they arrived.

"Good afternoon, Miss Harper," Amy said.

The young lady looked startled to see them. "Oh, good afternoon, my lord, my lady." Before they could say anything else, she hurried away.

William and Amy watched her weave in and out of the shoppers.

As they made their way through the stable door, Mr. Morris looked over from a metal piece he was working on. He wiped his hands on a cloth and greeted them. "How can I help you, my lord?"

Mr. Morris was an older man who had been the blacksmith for the village since William's childhood. He was a pleasant sort and kept himself busy with his metal and iron work, but as a hobby, he bought neglected weapons and restored them. One of his own firearms was the musket his great-grandfather had used in the Revolutionary War in America.

"I have a small gun collection of my own and wondered if you had something acquired recently that you were interested in parting with."

The man's eyes lit up. "You are a gun collector, also, my lord?"

William nodded. "Nothing like yours, of course."

Since guns were the man's favorite topic, he chattered on about various pieces displayed on the wall. William spent the time considering how to get him to answer a few questions. Before he could think of a way to do that, Amy said, "Mr. Morris, seeing these nicely displayed guns makes me think of the Harvest Festival we are planning for the fourteenth of October."

Certainly his wife was not going to ask the man to donate a gun?

"I was thinking about possibly having a shooting contest. What do you think?"

The man considered her words for a moment. "I don't know if that would be worth your time, my lady."

"Oh. Why is that?"

"Well, very few men that I know own guns. My collection has always been unique to the village."

Amy gave the man one of her sweet smiles. "And what about the ladies, Mr. Morris? For example, I just saw Miss Harper leaving your store. Is she one of your gun owners, too?"

"The young lady who was just in here? No. She wanted to sell a gun."

* * *

"THAT WAS QUITE an enlightening trip to the village," Amy said as they walked toward the carriage. "I can't help but wonder if Miss Harper tried to sell a gun to get rid of evidence or to get the money to provide for herself if she hasn't found employment yet."

William shook his head. "Actually, what I find quite odd is the fact that she owned a gun at all."

"Yes," she said. "Quite strange. Perhaps worth looking into."

He helped her into the carriage, and they returned home.

After arriving and handing their outerwear to Filbert, they headed upstairs to the nursery to visit Charles. And found Aunt Margaret there, watching Mrs. Grover change Charles' nappy.

She looked up as they entered. "I thought I would see how difficult this might be."

Amy grinned. "I've done it myself a few times. It's not too difficult. But I'm sure your nurse and nanny would be quite adept at keeping your babe clean and dry."

Aunt didn't respond to her comment about her nurse and nanny. Mrs. Grover lifted Charles. "Now you are all ready to visit with your mum and dad and auntie."

Amy took her sweet baby into her arms and cuddled him. "You smell so lovely."

"You may take a break now, Mrs. Grover. With three of us, I'm sure we can handle Charles for a while," William said.

Poor Charles became quite cranky after a short while, most

likely with the three adults passing him around for hugs and cuddles.

After about fifteen minutes, William stood and kissed Charles on the head. "I shall leave you ladies to enjoy my son. There is some work I need to do."

Aunt Margaret held Charles in her lap, which Amy thought was quite brave of her after the last time she did that. Although she was not jiggling him now.

Her aunt looked up at her. "Were you afraid when it got close to the time for Charles to be born?"

Amy thought for a moment, back to when she was nearing the end of her confinement. "I must admit I had some fears, but I had a great deal of faith in Dr. Stevens." Amy swiveled in her chair to face her aunt. "I do wish you were able to take advantage of Dr. Steven's expertise."

She ran her fingers through Charles' soft hair. "If Jonathan hasn't returned when my time grows near, I think I shall return to our house in Bath and look up this doctor you are so fond of."

"Then you would be alone!"

"Hmm. That is not a good idea, is it?"

Amy patted her hand. "Mrs. Townsend has a very good reputation in the village. She has delivered numerous babies, and everyone who has used her services was happy with her."

Aunt Margaret nodded and looked off, as if in deep thought.

They played with the baby for a while longer, then Mrs. Grover arrived. "I shall feed Charles his dinner now and bathe him for bed."

Amy hated surrendering him to the nurse, but she needed to get ready for dinner. "If the weather is nice tomorrow, I shall take Charles for a walk in his pram."

"That is a wonderful idea, my lady. He would enjoy that. Shall I plan on attending also?"

"No. I think I can handle my son for a couple of hours."

Mrs. Grover nodded. "Of course, you can. You are a wonderful mother."

She and Aunt Margaret left the nursery and when they reached the bedchamber floor, separated to prepare for dinner.

JUST AS AMY was ready to leave her room, there was a soft knock on the door. She opened it to see Mrs. Elliot standing there, clasping her hands tightly. "May I have a word with you, my lady?"

Amy stepped back. "Yes, please come in."

Mrs. Elliot opened and closed her mouth a few times before she spoke. "You and Lord Wethington are the most generous people I have ever met." She stopped and took a deep breath. "That is why I must tell you that Mr. Mackay has fully recovered from his illness."

"I am happy to hear that."

Mrs. Elliot waited for a moment, then said in a rush of words, "He is taking advantage of your good will, my lady. I don't think he has any intention of leaving the Manor. I must say the poor man has told me he has nowhere to go since he lived with his cousin who passed away recently, and her children told him he had to move because they were going to sell the house. Also, it doesn't sound as though his job will be waiting for him when he returns to Reading, but he is costing you money, as well as keeping me employed to take care of him."

Amy crossed her arms and thought for a minute. "Let me take this up with his lordship. In the meantime, do not trouble yourself with this. You seem to be distraught, and I don't want that." She patted her hand. "Why don't you get ready for dinner, and after I speak with Lord Wethington, I will let you know what we will do from here."

Mrs. Elliot let out a deep breath. "Thank you so much. I feel as though I've done my Christian duty by telling you this."

Amy stepped out the door. "That you have. I will see you downstairs."

This was indeed a problem. How could they send an old man back to Reading with nowhere to go?

The Colberts were already in the drawing room when Amy arrived.

"Would you care for a sherry, Amy?" Edward was apparently playing host until William appeared.

"Yes, I would, thank you."

Papa was next to enter. She had to admit since he'd been staying with them, he looked years younger. Her first thoughts were the lack of business stress since he'd told them he had turned most of the business over to Michael. But she had a feeling that Mrs. Elliot had something to do with it. It still amused her to see her papa acting as he did with the woman.

Persephone strutted into the room, took one look at the crowd of people, barked, and turned to leave.

Aunt Margaret raced into the room, almost tripping over the dog, tears coming down her face.

"What is wrong?" Amy asked, taking her in her arms.

She wiped her nose with a handkerchief. "Othello is dead." She placed her fingers over her lips. "He was only thirty-three years old. He should have lived much longer."

Lady Lily came over to them. "Oh, my dear. I am so sorry." She turned to Amy. "Who is Othello?"

"Her cockatoo."

"A bird?"

"Yes."

Her mother-in-law patted Aunt Margaret on her back and returned to her husband's side, mumbling something about disliking birds, then held out her glass for another sherry.

William entered the room and made a beeline for Amy. He

bent close to her ear. "We are getting quite crowded, are we not?"

"Shh. We don't want to embarrass anyone."

Mrs. Elliot was the next to join them, looking, as always, as if she didn't belong.

Papa, however, marched right over to her and took her hand and kissed it. "Good evening, Mrs. Elliot." He drew her forward. "Would you care for a sherry?"

"Thank you, Franklin, yes, I do believe I would like one tonight."

They all turned toward the doorway when Mr. Mackay strolled into the room as if he'd been there numerous times. He nodded at the others and addressed William. "Good evening, my lord. I thought I would save the lovely Mrs. Elliot from having to bring my tray upstairs. Since I was feeling a tad stronger today, I decided to join you down here."

William glanced over at Amy who shrugged and tried to hide her grin. Mr. Mackay rubbed his hands together and looked at Papa. "I don't mind having a sip of that brandy over there." He gestured toward the sideboard where the bottles of spirits sat.

Papa looked over at her. She nodded, and he poured a glass and handed the snifter to Mr. Mackay who held his glass up and said, "*Slainte!*"

"My lord, dinner is served."

Amy walked up to Filbert and lowered her voice. "Please have another place set at the dinner table for Mr. Mackay."

Without expression, he bowed. "I will do so immediately."

With the efficiency of their staff, by the time they all walked into the dining room, an additional place had been set.

It was a pleasant dinner of white soup, roasted fowl, stewed beef, and various vegetables. Mr. Mackay ate two helpings of everything, then joined them for a brandy in the library before Mrs. Elliot helped him upstairs.

With Papa following like a Buckingham Palace guard.

Within less than fifteen minutes, they had both returned to the library.

Aunt Margaret took a sip from her tea. "What about Othello?"

William cleared his throat. "What about him, Lady Margaret?"

"Doesn't anyone care? Except me?"

Amy walked over to where she sat and held her hand. "Of course, we all care. I know he meant a great deal to you, and you've had him for a long time."

Her aunt took out her handkerchief and patted her eyes. "Yes."

Mrs. Elliot joined them where Amy and Aunt Margaret sat, looking quite sympathetic. "Who is Othello? A friend of yours?"

"My cockatoo."

Mrs. Elliot looked at Amy. "A bird?"

"Yes."

"Oh." She patted Aunt Margaret's back. "I'm sure he had a good life." She rose and joined Papa.

Amy continued to hold Aunt Margaret's hand. "What do you want done with him?" The last thing they needed with everything going on was a dead bird smelling up the house.

"I shall hold a funeral for him tomorrow." She wiped her nose. "May I bury him in your garden? Near the roses?"

Amy paled at the idea of telling their gardener, Dawson, that Aunt Margaret wanted to dig up part of the rose garden to bury a dead bird. "I shall speak to Dawson first thing in the morning."

"Thank you." She placed her teacup on the table in front of her. "I shall retire now. It's been a most stressful day."

"I think we shall make our way up to our bedchamber also," Lady Lily said. "We have more work to do in the bookstore."

"Are you close to opening?" William asked.

"I think so. We will know more tomorrow after we spend time there." Lady Lily looked at Amy. "My tearoom is all set up." The woman glowed.

"That is wonderful news. I am so delighted for you."

That left just Papa and Mrs. Elliot in the room with them. Once they departed the library, William took her hand in his. "With everyone retiring early, perhaps that's the best thing for us to do as well."

"Yes. I have a wonderful book I just started."

He wrapped his arm around her waist and moved her forward. "Ah, my love, I have a better idea."

"WHAT THE DEVIL time is it that someone is pounding on the front door?" William asked as he sat up in bed.

Amy rolled over and yawned. "Whatever time it is, it is too early." She rolled back over.

Within minutes, there was a knock on their bedchamber door. "My lord. Your presence is requested downstairs."

Amy rolled back over and sat up. "Whatever could that mean?"

William glanced at the pink and white China clock across the room "It's barely six o'clock."

"Who is here?" he asked Filbert through the door as he tugged on his trousers.

"Mr. Morris, my lord."

"The man can't be that anxious to sell me a gun," William muttered as he grabbed his dressing gown. Just as he reached for his shoes, Amy jumped from the bed.

"I'm going with you."

He nodded and slipped his shoes on. "We shall be down momentarily," he said through the door.

Amy was dressed in a few minutes, two different shoes,

161

misbuttoned dressing gown, and her hair not brushed, but the mass of curls fastened at her nape. "I am ready."

Mr. Morris awaited them in the drawing room. When they entered, he was pacing, then turned and bowed briefly. "My lord, I have bad news and I knew not what to do, so as our lord, I decided to see you."

"What is it, Morris?"

The man paled and swallowed a couple of times. "I was out walking in the woods early this morning and stumbled across Mr. Reynolds' dead body."

"Shot?" William said.

He nodded. "Yes. In the head."

*a*my sat on the settee, her breath leaving her body. Another murder? She'd thought once they left Bath behind the murders would cease. Her stomach did a flip, and she looked up at William, still speaking to Mr. Morris. Their voices grew dim and everything else faded.

She reached her hand out. "William."

She woke up stretched out on the settee. William sat next to her, applying a cold cloth to her forehead. Mrs. O'Sullivan hovered over her. "Ah, good, my lord. She is awake."

"Don't try to get up just yet," William said. "You've had a shock, and I think it's best if you give your body time to recover."

She looked around the room. It almost seemed like a dream. More a nightmare.

William continued to move his finger up and down her cheek. "Mrs. O'Sullivan, can you mix up a tisane for her ladyship?"

Amy shook her head. "No. That will just make me sleep. I prefer a good cup of tea."

William nodded, and the housekeeper left the room.

"Do you think Mr. Reynolds's murder is connected to the vicar's?" She struggled to sit up, and William helped her so she was leaning against the back of the settee.

"Since the village has not been afflicted with murders in the past that I am aware of, it seems likely they are connected. How, I have no idea."

Amy looked past William's shoulder. "I see Mr. Morris has left."

"Yes. He was somewhat disconcerted. I thought he might be the next one to faint."

"I don't faint."

Another murder. Different setting, different method. It would seem to be not connected, but how likely would it be for a quiet village to have two murders in less than two weeks? "They must be connected, William. It is up to us to figure it out."

"Not so." William stood and paced. "We are going to visit the Magistrate again. I will demand he assign a constable for this village—something I've been asking for. My multiple requests have been ignored. The constable can start an investigation into both murders."

Mrs. O'Sullivan carried in a small tray with a teapot, cup and saucer, and sugar and cream. She placed it on the table in front of her. "Do you wish to have some breakfast, my lady?"

"No. My stomach is not doing well this morning. The tea is just what I need."

William walked to the small desk in the drawing room. He withdrew a piece of paper and began to write. Once he was finished, he summoned Filbert, who answered his bidding fully dressed for the day. "Yes, my lord?"

"I want this delivered immediately to the Magistrate in Reading. Benson knows where it is since he drove us there. Have him take one of the horses instead of the carriage."

Filbert took the missive from William's hand.

"What does the letter say?" Amy asked as she sipped her tea.

"I told Sir Archibald that we will visit him this afternoon and we expect to have him ready to send a permanent constable to Wethingford. I also mentioned that there has been another murder."

"Hopefully that will gain his notice and have him do something to help." Amy placed her teacup in the saucer. "We will need to send a note to Mr. Graves and have him remove the body."

"Not just yet. I want to have a look at the area. Perhaps we can ask Lady Margaret to do a sketch for us."

"That's an excellent idea. We really should obtain one of those new cameras. That would help in times like this."

William sat alongside her, his features concerned as he took her hands in his. "They are too new. I'm not sure they are worth the investment just yet. I think Lady Margaret would do a much better job."

"If she is willing to sketch a dead body. And she is planning on Othello's burial today."

William reared back. "Surely she's not planning any type of a funeral?"

"I don't know, but one of us has to speak with Dawson about digging up a patch of the rose garden to put Othello in there."

He sighed. "Amy, do you remember when it was just the three of us? Me, you, and Charles?"

"And dozens of staff."

"Yes. But now we have Lady Margaret, my parents, your father, Mr. MacKay, and Mrs. Elliot."

She sighed. "I know, but I do like having family around. They all get along fairly well, and it gives me company during the day when you are overtaxed with estate matters."

"Speaking of estate matters, I do have something that needs to be done this morning. Why don't you speak with

Dawson when you are dressed and arrange for the bird's burial."

Amy nodded. "And I will ask Aunt Margaret about doing a sketch of Mr. Reynolds' body and the area around it."

"I want to be there when she does it." He stood and reached his hand out. "Come, let us get dressed and spend the day dealing with another murder."

* * *

IT TOOK a bit of soothing ruffled feathers to have Dawson agree to dig up a small part of the garden for Othello. Aunt Margaret agreed to sketch Mr. Reynolds if she could have Othello buried in the rose garden, so it had all worked out.

Amy had to postpone her promise to take Charles for a ride in his pram since the situation with the bird had taken up a good portion of the morning. With a kiss on his head and an assurance to take him for a stroll the next morning, she left, feeling like a bad mother.

Amy had agreed to meet William after luncheon in her solar. Aunt Margaret was with her, holding her sketch book. Still sniffling from Othello's burial.

"Are we ready, ladies?" William entered the room, Mr. Morris behind him.

"Yes." Amy stood and shook out her skirts.

Mr. Morris was to guide them to the spot where he found Mr. Reynolds' body. Mr. Graves would meet them at the edge of the woods with the vehicle he used for picking up bodies and transporting them to the burial site.

Since the carriage was ready to take them to Reading once this procedure was over, they decided to ride to the woods instead of walking. William, Amy, Aunt Margaret, and Mr. Morris all climbed into the vehicle.

It was a somber group that gathered at the edge of the

woods. Word had spread in the village, so there were a few onlookers, mumbling to each other.

Once they left the carriage, they formed a line with Mr. Morris leading them. Aunt Margaret followed, then Mr. Graves, carrying a stretcher, and then William and Amy, holding hands.

"I must admit, I'm a bit squeamish about seeing his corpse." She looked up at William. "I know I've done this before, but my body has changed a bit since Charles was born. And lately, it's been giving me even more trouble."

"I will be happy to walk you back to the carriage. You don't have to do this, and you will have Lady Margaret's sketch to look at if you are curious."

"No. If she can stand to sketch the body, I can stand to look at it."

He eyed her skeptically. "You won't faint on me again, will you?"

"I don't faint."

"Ah, yes. I forgot." He put his arm around her shoulders and hugged her close. "In the off chance you should swoon, however, I will catch you."

She sniffed, and they continued forward.

At last they came to the body. Mr. Morris waved in the direction and stepped back. He did look a tad green. Amy took a brief look and then turned away, her stomach roiling.

Aunt Margaret swallowed several times, and with determination, began to sketch. Once she was finished, William asked her to sketch the area around the body while he looked for footprints.

"There are just too many leaves to actually see imprints," William said.

"Are we finished now?" Mr. Graves asked.

William nodded, not looking too hardy himself. "Yes."

"I'll need one of you blokes to help me put the man on the stretcher and then carry him to my cart."

Since Mr. Morris had already left the area, William stepped up. "I will help you." He turned to Amy and Aunt Margaret. "Why don't you ladies go on ahead to the carriage. I will be with your shortly."

With a sigh of relief, they departed, arms linked.

* * *

WILLIAM KNEELED and examined the hole in Reynolds' head. A clear shot to his forehead, which meant he was most likely facing his killer when it happened. Why would he meet someone in the woods? It could have been accidental, but William was sure this had been a planned encounter.

The man was pale and cold. Blood was scattered around the hole in his forehead.

"Can you tell how long he's been dead?" He really didn't know if Mr. Graves had any sort of training, but dealing with dead bodies all the time, he certainly knew more than William did.

"I'd say at least twelve hours for his body to be this cool and in this stage of rigor mortis."

He and Mr. Graves lifted the body, and William thought about the phrase 'dead weight'. He was a big man, hefty. It took all their effort to move him from the ground to the stretcher.

Once he was on the stretcher, it was much easier to carry the body. William helped Mr. Graves slide the stretcher into the back of his cart. "You have someone to help you when you get to your store?"

"Yes. My son is a strong one. He'll get the bloke into the room so I can get him ready for burial."

William remembered that Jane Hamilton needed to be notified about her father's death. He shook off the feeling that her husband, Joseph, might have been the one to commit the crime. Once he and Amy have spoken to the Magistrate, they would have to put their heads together and try to figure this out. Hopefully, whoever Sir Archibald sends to act as constable will have some experience.

When they'd asked Mr. Mackay to accompany them as the so-called coroner, he began to cough and said he wasn't feeling well and a trek into the woods would just make his *ague* return.

It was a quiet ride from the woods to the Manor. William reviewed the sketch Lady Margaret had done, then studied both women who looked a tad pale. When they pulled up in front of the Manor, Lady Margaret left, and William took Amy's hand. "Do you want me to go to Reading alone? You look a little pale."

"No. I'm fine." She shook her head and smiled. "Let's go so we can return in time for dinner."

On the way to Reading, William's thoughts were consumed with Mr. Reynolds. He was not a well-liked man, and he had made a few people angry enough to threaten him. But what could possibly be the connection between the murder of a well-liked vicar and a very unpopular man?

If they were connected. But two random murders just didn't sit well with him, especially since the method was the same.

When they arrived at the Magistrate's office, they encountered the same officer at the front desk as the last time.

"I assume you are here to see Sir Archibald, my lord?"

"Yes. He should have received a note this morning advising him that we would be here this afternoon to discuss a very serious situation."

"Yes," the young man said. "I have been advised to bring you to his office once you arrived." He gestured toward the corridor. "Please follow me."

The young officer gave a slight knock and then opened the

door, waving them in. Sir Archibald stood as they entered. "Good afternoon, my lord, my lady. You are both looking well." He gestured to the two chairs in front of his desk "Please have a seat."

Once they were all settled, the Magistrate placed his hands on his desk, his fingers interlocked. "Am I to understand from the note you sent earlier that there has been another murder in Wethingford?"

William leaned back in his chair and rested his foot on his knee. "That is correct. We have not uncovered the murderer in the first incident yet." He leaned forward. "We need someone assigned to our village who has the ability to deal with this situation. I have asked repeatedly for this, and nothing has happened."

"I understand," the man said. "How helpful has Mr. Mackay been?"

William and Amy looked at each other. Amy cleared her throat. "I believe we sent along information to you that the man was sick with an *ague*."

"Yes. I remember. Is he feeling better? It has been some time."

"He apparently has some good days and some bad days." William crossed his arms over his chest. "We need another person. An officer of the law. Someone who can unravel this mess and get it straightened out. Then stay in our village as the assigned Village Constable. I don't think that is too much to ask."

Sir Archibald shook his head. "No. It is time. I have someone I'm assigning to your village. He is packed and ready to go with you when you return home this afternoon. If you excuse me for a moment, I will summon him."

William took a deep breath and sat back. "This sounds promising."

Within minutes Sir Archibald had returned with a man—

quite young—who nodded to them, then stood at attention. "My lord, my lady, I am Officer Richard Wheeler. I am honored to be assigned to Wethingford."

"Thank you," William said.

"I am ready to leave at a moment's notice, my lord."

"Wonderful," Amy added.

"Just say the word, my lord."

William stood, feeling like he should. "Well, then, I guess we will be on our way."

Sir Archibald rose to his feet. "I assume you will provide a place for Mr. Wheeler to stay until he can secure lodgings for himself?"

"Of course," Amy said, a bright smile on her face. "We have plenty of room." William swore she mumbled under her breath, "Soon William and I, and our poor child will be forced to move to the stables."

The Magistrate walked around his desk and slapped William on the back. "I'm sure Wheeler will do a wonderful job for you."

"What about Mr. Mackay?"

Sir Archibald pushed William forward, toward the office door. "He can stay and help Wheeler out." He kept his hand on the latch of his door as William, Amy, and Wheeler left the office.

"Send me a report," he said before closing the door.

Wheeler lifted a satchel and stood straight again as if facing his commanding officer. "I am prepared to do an exceptional job for you, my lord."

William already felt worn out by the man, and they hadn't even left the Magistrate's office.

"The dinner table is getting more crowded by the day," Amy said as they left the building.

"Indeed."

18

"William, what are we going to do about Mr. Mackay? Mrs. Elliot is concerned that she's costing us money because we hired her to take care of him and he is recovered. She said he spent yesterday afternoon strolling around the garden, then read for a couple of hours in the library. He joined Mrs. Elliot, Aunt Margaret, Eloise, and me for tea and asked to have his clothing cleaned and pressed so he would look more presentable."

William laughed until his eyes watered.

"What is so funny? Mrs. Elliot is very concerned."

"My dear wife. I pay the bills and I am not concerned. If Mrs. Elliot wants to stay busy so she feels as though she is earning her keep, have her join my mother at the bookstore. She can help finish the setup and then put a few hours in a week to work at the store."

"That's a wonderful idea! We said when Mr. Mackay was recovered we would find something for her to do, and that is the perfect solution." She stopped for few moments. "Although I had hoped to have your mother employ Miss Harper. If she is selling personal items to keep a roof over her head, the poor girl needs a job."

William pulled her into his arms. "You are so very soft-hearted, my love."

"As are you," she returned.

"Aye. Perhaps we will one day find ourselves in the poorhouse."

She eyed him skeptically. "If money is a problem, I have all my royalties that Michael has been keeping and investing for the years I've been writing."

He shook his head and pushed a loose strand of hair behind her ear. "It is my duty to provide shelter, feed and clothe you and Charles. And anyone else who resides in our home, temporarily or permanently. I do not need, nor want, your money. We had already decided to save that for the benefit of our children."

Amy smirked. "You are so very rich, then?"

"*We* are not so *very* rich. But *we* do not need to concern ourselves with how many mouths we must feed."

She nodded. "Good. I had hoped to send Charles to Eton and then University."

"Good grief, Amy, let the lad grow out of his nappies first."

"Are you ready for the funeral?" Aunt Margaret walked into the drawing room, tugging her gloves on.

Amy moved out of William's arms and sighed. "Yes. I am ready."

It was two days after Mr. Reynolds' body had been found. Mr. Wheeler had settled in quite nicely and made a visit to Mr. Graves to view the body. Mr. Graves reported that the young man took one look at Reynolds, turned a lovely shade of green, left the building, and emptied his stomach on the front lawn.

With Mrs. Elliot's situation taken care of, Mr. Mackay was enjoying his golden years with walks in the garden, devouring the books in the library, and drinking William's fine whisky.

He never mentioned leaving.

And no one asked.

Papa was thrilled that Mr. Mackay's recovery did not influence Mrs. Elliot's status as a guest in the house. Amy had a feeling he would have quite a bit to say if that happened.

They were all gathering in the drawing room to leave for the funeral. William had Benson take out the second carriage that was seldom used because there were so many from the Manor heading to the church.

Amy, William, the Colberts, and Mr. Wheeler rode in one carriage. Aunt Margaret, Papa, Mrs. Elliot, and Mr. Mackay in the other.

The vicar had cancelled the Sunday Service the day before, stating that preparations for the funeral the next day would take up too much of his time. Although Amy thought that odd, they really didn't know Mr. Hopkins that well, so perhaps that was a normal thing for him.

Despite Reynolds being an unpopular man, the church was filled. But then the notoriety of another murder must have drawn even more than the vicar's death. And there was always the luncheon that followed these affairs.

Mr. Hopkins walked to the front of the sanctuary looking somber. He closed his eyes for a moment and slowly shook his head. "I did not know the gentleman we are honoring today." He paused and looked up at the heavens before glancing at William. "Therefore, I feel the Lord is asking me to have Lord Wethington say a few words about Mr. Reynolds."

Amy leaned over. "Were you expecting this?"

"No. And the only thing I have to say about Reynolds was how disliked he was."

She patted his hand. "Do your best."

Calling on his experience with Parliamentary orations, William managed to speak about a man who no one liked, and

175

he didn't really know and made him sound like a candidate for God's final reward.

He'd leave the decision up to God in which direction Reynolds' reward was.

The vicar invited those who wished to join him at the grave site for the interment to step outside. The others could go directly to Fellowship Hall for the luncheon.

Maybe because it was the new vicar's first funeral or the morbid sense of the man's death, most of the attendees arranged themselves around the grave.

Heads bowed, the vicar opened his prayer book and began: "Dearly beloved we are gathered here to join this man and this woman…"

Amy looked over at William and frowned. "What?" she mouthed.

William stepped up to the vicar. "Mr. Hopkins, I believe you are reading the wrong pages of your prayer book."

For a moment he looked confused, then flipped the pages. "Yes. Of course. I marked it last night." He laughed. "Wrong marker."

He started again amid giggles and a lot of clearing of throats.

Amy was holding in her laughter so hard she thought she would burst. At the very least she would snort which is what she'd done as a girl when she was trying to keep from laughing in school. She took a deep breath and avoided looking at Aunt Margaret since she knew her control would vanish.

Fortunately, the prayers he read were quite simple and fast. He bowed his head and murmured, "Amen," and then closed his book. "We may now all depart and make our way to Fellowship Hall."

Aunt Margaret walked up to her and linked their arms. "Did Mr. Hopkins begin reading the marriage ceremony?"

"Yes. I'm afraid he did. I think it might be that he was a bit disconcerted, this being his first funeral here and not knowing anyone."

Aunt Margaret studied her. "You are much too kind, Niece."

Well, so far this morning she'd been called softhearted and kind. While she thought those words were meant as a reproach, she felt quite proud of being kind and softhearted.

The hall was bursting with congregants. The various scents of food placed carefully along two very long tables would normally entice her to eat, but the mixture was making her stomach churn instead. Two funerals in a couple of weeks would do that to one.

Their group managed to find seats near each other. Mr. Mackay sat across from Amy and looked around, rubbing his hands together. "Everything smells good." He turned and twisted in his chair. "I wonder if they have whisky."

"I don't think so, Mr. Mackay. You won't find spirits in church," Amy said.

Mr. Wheeler had taken the seat next to Amy. He leaned down and said, "I will walk around the hall and see if anyone looks guilty."

It was quite frightening that his statement was the most intelligent thing they'd heard from him since he'd arrived. He had settled nicely into his room, which was small since they wanted to keep all the guests close together to make it easier for the maids to do their job. Unfortunately, the only room left in that wing was smaller than the others, but Mr. Wheeler seemed quite pleased with it.

He'd spent all day Sunday in the village, introducing himself as the new constable. So far, she hadn't heard from anyone about Mr. Wheeler.

What she and William needed to do was speak to a few people themselves. Mr. Granger came to mind, as well as Miss Harper. They also had never established why Mr. Fletcher was in Mr. Smythe's appointment book every week. Mr. Reynolds had been at the top of their list for the vicar's murder, but she doubted that he had shot himself. So, if there were two murderers, one of them was dead.

Certainly, Joseph Hamilton, with the dislike he had for his father-in-law, could have killed Mr. Reynolds, but the way he protectively cared for his wife during the funeral service made it seem unlikely that he could callously kill her father. Especially since there was no reason to believe his marriage to Jane would be annulled.

She started to get a headache from all her mental wanderings.

"William, I would like to visit Miss Harper. I haven't seen her yet this morning, so I'm assuming since she's new to the village, she didn't know Mr. Reynolds and had no reason to attend his funeral. But first I want to speak with your mother about the possibility of Miss Harper working at the bookstore."

"That sounds like a good idea." His eyes wandered to where Mr. Wheeler stood speaking with Mr. Morris, both enjoying a laugh. "It appears Mr. Wheeler will not be any more help than Mr. Mackay, but being so young, there's a good chance he's never been faced with a murder before. Maybe he will be much better as a constable. Keeping the peace and all."

She stood. "I want to speak with your mother for a minute."

William nodded and was immediately taken up with Mr. Gabel who sat next to him.

Mrs. Gabel stood and addressed Amy. "My lady, I know this is a delicate time with two murders in our village." She shuddered. "But is it possible to have another meeting this week on the Harvest Festival? Since it grows near, we just need to tie a few things up and we really appreciate your input."

"Yes. That would be fine. Say, Wednesday for tea? About three o'clock?"

Mrs. Gabel bobbed. "Thank you so much, my lady, I will tell the other women."

Amy wondered if it was improper to hold a Festival with two men murdered and no one under arrest. Would some of the villagers, especially the women, feel safe enough to participate?

She shook off her morbid thoughts and headed to where Lady Lily was in a deep conversation with her husband.

* * *

LATER THAT DAY, William and Amy once again sat at a table at the Inn with Lucy—as usual—running around the room, trying to keep everyone happy. Amy noticed that most of the patrons were merely drinking, very little food being served. That made sense if they were just coming from the funeral where there had been a great deal of food.

"My lord, my lady, what a surprise to see you here." Mr. Wheeler stood at their table, eying the empty chair.

"Won't you join us, Mr. Wheeler," William said.

"Thank you." He pulled out the chair and sat, then leaned in and looked around the room. "Someone here is our murderer."

Amy glanced at William and said, "Have you identified him yet?"

"No. But you can see who it is by studying their faces. They will show relief since they haven't been caught."

William ran his hand down his face. "That is how you determine who committed murder? Has that worked in the past?"

Wheeler shook his head. "No. This is my first murder case."

William waved at Lucy to bring him another drink.

"Do you see that man over there in the gray jacket and trousers?" He gestured behind them.

"Yes. I see him."

"He looks guilty to me."

William sighed. "That is Mr. Lawrence. He must be eighty

years old. He couldn't hit the side of a barn with his poor eyesight."

Wheeler smiled. "Ah, but I didn't mean guilty for the murder. But he is guilty for something."

Amy felt like she was sitting in Bedlam. "Mr. Wheeler, I think perhaps it might be a better idea to visit the site where Mr. Reynolds was found and study the sketch Lady Margaret did of the body and area around it. You might find some clues there."

"An excellent idea, my lady!" He stood, bowed, and marched out of the room.

Lucy walked up to their table. "Who is that man?"

"He is the village's new constable."

She shook her head and hurried off.

They had sent off a note asking Joseph Hamilton to join them at the Inn. They felt it was a better idea to talk here instead of their home where Jane was grieving.

The door opened and Joseph entered. He looked around and headed to their table. He slumped into the chair and ran his fingers through his hair. "It has been a tough day, my lord."

"The funeral?" William asked.

"Yes. And my wife." He waved at Lucy. "No matter how difficult Reynolds was to live with, even to be around, he was still Jane's father. And to die in such a horrible way is just tearing her apart."

Amy reached across the table and covered the man's hand with hers. "I understand. There is a bond between parents and children that rarely breaks."

Lucy delivered a tankard of ale to Joseph. He smiled and nodded his thanks.

It reminded Amy that he was such a nice young man. But—with the threat of annulment hanging over his head, even if it was unlikely—would that give him leave to kill Mr. Reynolds?

But shooting the vicar? What would be his motive for that? He was the man who had stood up for him.

Again, she was linking the two murders together. But no other scenario seemed likely.

Joseph wiped the liquid from his mouth with the sleeve of his shirt. "So, then I told Jane to prepare a tisane and try to sleep."

Amy realized she had missed what Joseph had said, but William would pass along any worthwhile information.

"I will pay her a visit this week," Amy said. "Maybe getting her involved in the upcoming Harvest Festival will cheer her up."

Joseph nodded and then finished the rest of his drink. "I must return now. I missed my morning work because of the funeral, so I need to catch up." He stood and nodded at them and left the Inn.

"What do you think?" Amy asked.

William took a deep breath. "He is genuinely concerned about this wife. And I understand her pain. For as difficult as Reynolds was, there must have been some warmth between them."

Lucy walked up to their table. "Now that I have a minute, there is something I wanted to talk to you about." She looked over her shoulder in the direction of the kitchen, most likely waiting to be called for some duty.

"Mr. Fletcher and Mr. Reynolds were playing cards here the other night. They got into an argument because Mr. Reynolds accused Mr. Fletcher of cheating. They stood and the argument grew quite loud. Just as my da came out of the kitchen, Mr. Reynolds drew back his arm to swing at Mr. Fletcher, who pulled out a knife and said something to the effect that he should be careful with making threats like that lest he end up dead."

19

"It appears we have a connection between the two murders. Although we have no idea yet why Mr. Fletcher was written in Mr. Smythe's appointment book, he might be the one to break into the vicar's office," William said as they crossed the green headed to the bookstore.

"And now we know he pulled a knife and threatened Reynolds just a day or so before he was murdered."

"However, Reynolds wasn't stabbed, but shot."

They entered the bookstore, a slight tinkle from the bell on the top of the door announcing their arrival. His mother looked up from where she directed one of his maids to adjust the curtains in the back of the store area that she'd designated her tearoom.

"Lady Lily," Amy said as she walked over to the space. "That looks just lovely."

His mother turned and grinned. "Doesn't it, dear? I am so happy with how this has all come together."

"It appears you are almost ready to open," William said as he looked around the store.

Painters had been hired to repaint, and it had brought a

whole new brightness to the area. William had sent his two footmen, Carter and Lyons, to move the bookcases into a new arrangement that looked much more pleasing to the eye.

Mrs. Elliot was adding books to the shelves according to the Dewey decimal system that most bookstores had adopted. Annabelle's Attic had not been one of them, but apparently Edward was using the system because Mrs. Elliot kept glancing at a piece of paper outlining where each title should be shelved.

His mother thanked the maid and turned her attention to him. "I have hired Mrs. Elliot permanently for a few half days a week. I did offer her more than a few days, but Lord Winchester told me last evening that Mrs. Elliot did not need to work more than a few hours a week."

Amy glanced at William, her brows raised.

"I also offered a job to the lovely Miss Harper, who was thrilled. Because she is on her own, I gave her five days a week."

"When is opening day?" Amy asked.

"I had thought about the night of the Harvest Festival, but since that is over a week away, I will do it sooner. Perhaps this weekend."

"You should see Mr. Penrose over at the printing shop," William said. "He could prepare several handbills for you to distribute to various stores."

"That is an excellent idea!"

Mrs. Elliot walked up to them. "Excuse me, my lord, but I think a small banner draped in the front store window would be a nice touch also."

"Yes," Lady Lily said.

"I could do it for you. I did seamstress work for years," Mrs. Elliot said. "I will purchase some cloth and stitch some wording on there for you."

His mother shook her head. "I love the idea, but I will purchase the cloth. If you go to the Sundry Shop and pick out what you think would look best, ask Mr. Granger to put it on Mr. Colbert's bill."

As Mrs. Elliot walked back to her work of shelving the books, his mother said, "She is truly a lovely lady. So helpful."

"Yes, I trust Franklin believes so, too." William grinned. "But I don't necessarily imagine his interest in her is because of her helpfulness."

"A nice touch would be to have Cook prepare some small cakes for the opening to give out to people to encourage them to come into the bookstore," Amy said.

His mother hugged Amy. "Such marvelous ideas. I am so glad you stopped in for a visit."

William placed his hand on Amy's shoulder. "We will be on our way and see you at dinner."

They left the store and headed home. It was such a pleasant day that they had passed on having the carriage.

Once they passed the stables, Amy put her hand out. "Wait just a minute, William."

"What is the matter? You look quite pale."

"That ale we had at the Inn didn't sit well. I feel a bit queasy. I think just a short rest will restore me."

William frowned. "Perhaps you should see Dr. Evans. Your stomach has been giving you trouble for a while now."

Amy shook her head. "No. I'm fine, just a sensitive stomach lately." She grinned at him. "Perhaps I am merely growing old."

"Never say! I'm older than you, and I don't expect to reach my dotage for many years."

* * *

AMY SPENT all day Tuesday and part of Wednesday taking Charles on the promised pram ride and working on her book. With the distraction of two real murders on her mind, she was finding it hard to work out the pretend murders.

She'd spent the last half hour admiring the lovely cakes and sandwiches Cook had prepared for her meeting on the Harvest Festival. After a quick visit to the nursery, she left word with Filbert to bring the ladies directly upstairs.

William had gone out, mumbling something about a meeting, but she thought he was merely escaping the house with all the ladies arriving. The Manor was certainly large enough, but she was sure the more distance he could put between the ladies and himself, the better.

Eloise, who had decided to join the women doing the Harvest Festival, was the first to arrive, rushing in as usual, out of breath. "Was Mr. Reynolds' funeral this week?" she asked as she took her seat next to Amy.

"Monday. It was a quick one because it seems all of Vicar Hopkins' services are fast. Jane, of course, was there with her husband Joseph. He was concerned about her."

"Is she in a family way?"

Amy looked surprised. "I don't know. But now I wonder if that is so since she was quite distraught at the funeral, and I'm not sure her relationship with her father deserved all her grief." Amy hesitated for a moment. "Something odd happened at the funeral."

"What is that?"

"When we got to the grave site, the new vicar began the ceremony of interment by reading from his prayer book the marriage ceremony."

Eloise choked. "Sister, I think you are funning me."

Amy shook her head. "No. I nudged William, and he stepped up and told the vicar he was reading the wrong page. I imagine facing all those new people, conducting a funeral for the first time after just arriving, must have flustered him."

"If I had been there, I think I would have burst out laughing."

Amy smiled. "I almost did. But I'm sure it would have embarrassed the poor man."

"Lady Wethington, what a pleasure to see you. And you as well, Lady Davenport." The ladies had arrived altogether.

After a considerable amount of air kissing and exclaiming over hats and dresses, they all settled down minutes before Carter pushed in the tea tray.

Aunt Margaret entered the room, looking a tad fatigued and again not exactly put together as she normally would be. "I'm sorry, I hope I didn't hold up the meeting. I was playing with Charles and lost track of time."

Eloise nudged Amy in the ribs. "Playing with Charles?" she whispered.

"I know. Isn't it strange?"

Luckily all the women were talking at once so Aunt Margaret didn't hear their conversation. Amy and Eloise passed around the tea and plates so the ladies could help themselves to the offerings.

Once they'd all taken their last sips of tea, Amy clapped her hands to get their attention. "Ladies, an exciting thing I wish to announce. Lady Lily is close to opening her bookstore."

"That's wonderful," Mrs. Gabel said. "I just know it will be a very nice place."

"Oh, it is. She has even made a formal tea area for the ladies to sit and enjoy tea and browse the books."

"It sounds as though your mother-in-law has quite the head for business."

Amy smiled. "I agree. She is a woman who spent her entire life being waited on and cared for. Now she is like an impresario when it comes to her ability to see things that would make the bookstore better. Who would have thought a Lady would have such business acuity?"

"I am not surprised," Mrs. Waters said. She sniffed. "I think women's abilities are very underrated."

The women all stared at her in silence. "Yes. I am a forward-thinking woman. Men have ruled the world so far, and they've made a mess of things in my opinion."

The women all nodded, and Amy said, "You are so correct, Mrs. Waters. I was forced to write under a pen name because my father didn't approve of me writing murder mysteries because I am a woman!"

Mrs. Gabel looked at her. "But everyone knows you are the author E. D. Burton. Did your father eventually concede?"

Amy smiled. "No. When Lord Wethington proposed to me, I made it a condition of my acceptance that he allow me to reveal myself."

The women burst into peals of laughter.

"That is wonderful," Miss Martin said. "But what would you have done if he didn't agree?"

"I was very sure he would, but if he hadn't," she stopped and pretended to consider that. "I would have married him anyway and changed his mind." She winked at the group. "There are ways, you know."

Miss Martin turned a bright red. "I don't believe I should be part of this conversation."

Again, laughter erupted.

"Yet women run their households, maintain the household accounts, and balance children, and in many cases, numerous tasks around the house," Mrs. Applegate said, returning to the original conversation.

"I believe when the Harvest Festival is over, we should organize a group of women in the village to discuss this. There are many women around the country who feel as we do and there are many groups forming."

"It is certainly something to consider," Eloise said.

Mrs. Gabel took in a deep breath. "Do you know, Lady Wethington, if Mr. Reynolds' murderer has been found?"

Before Amy answered, Miss Martin said, "And Mr.

Smythe's murderer." She looked around at the other ladies. "I must admit I am feeling nervous when I'm home alone. Especially at night. I had Mr. Morris make me a new lock for my door."

"Mr. Morris the blacksmith? I didn't realize he made locks," Mrs. Applegate said. "Perhaps I will approach him to make a lock for my house."

"Mr. Morris is a nice man, but I must admit he makes me nervous," Mrs. Waters said. "He is so large and muscular. There is something about him that makes me glad I don't have to deal with him much."

"Yes, he is intimidating." Mrs. Applegate shuddered.

"I thought we had a new constable. Mr. Wheeler, I believe? Is he searching for the killers?" Mrs. Applegate shivered.

"He must be. He stopped in at my husband's butcher's shop and asked a great deal of questions," Mrs. Waters said. "But David said he didn't seem to ask questions that made any sense."

Amy made another mental note to speak with Mr. Wheeler also. As inept as he seemed, he still might have picked up some information that Amy and William could use. "Ladies, I suggest we get on with our meeting about the Harvest Festival, which is coming up soon."

Everyone started speaking at once, and the meeting continued.

* * *

WILLIAM SAT IN HIS STUDY, going over the numbers his steward had given him for the tenant rents he had collected. He hadn't raised the rent on his tenants since he'd taken over when his father had died. That was over fifteen years ago. His steward had been strongly suggesting that it was time to do so, but since the farms were productive and they paid part of their rent with food for the Manor, he just didn't feel the need to raise their payment.

Of course, like all the major estates, he'd lost some tenants when they moved to the city for industrial jobs, but his financial investments were paying off well and his overall situation was solid. If things continued as they were, he was reluctant to put the burden of a higher rent on them.

A slight knock on the study door drew his attention. Franklin stuck his head in. "Do you have a minute, William?"

"I do. And I'm glad for the interruption." He threw his pencil down on the desk. "My eyes are glazing over looking at rows and rows of numbers."

"I have just met with my solicitor who was gracious enough to come from Bath to assist me in the purchase of a house here in the village."

William's brows rose. "Indeed. And with all the estates you own, why buy a house in the village?"

Franklin took a deep breath and looked almost sheepish, which was more startling than buying another property. "I intend to propose to Mrs. Elliot, and she wants to stay here in the village where she's lived her entire life."

William grinned. "I believe congratulations are in order, Franklin. I can't say I am totally surprised by this, and I wish you both years of happiness."

His father-in-law leaned forward. "What do you suppose Amy and Michael will think of this? I mean, here I am in my golden years, and I'm marrying for the second time after being single for more than seventeen years." He shook his head. "There is something about Mrs. Elliot that fascinated me from the time I met her."

"Again, that is not something I find surprising and I'm sure your children won't either. Remember, my mother only remarried a couple of years ago as well."

William thought of how his mother told him Franklin

didn't want Mrs. Elliot to work too many hours. He suspected at the time that there was a reason for his request, and it appeared he was correct.

"Where is the house you purchased?"

"I preferred to have one built, but I didn't want to postpone the wedding for as long as it would take to build, especially with the bad weather upon us." Seeming more comfortable now, Franklin leaned back in his seat, his legs crossed. "My solicitor somehow came up with a man who very recently purchased a house and has decided a small village was not for him, so he wanted to sell it. His name is Mr. Kenneth Walsh, third son of Lord Maurice Lawton. He mentioned he met you and Amy at the Inn when he first arrived."

"Yes. I remember him." William not only remembered the man but found it odd that he bought a house just when two murders were committed and was now selling it.

20

Franklin chose that evening to announce to the family that he had offered his hand in marriage to Mrs. Elliot, and she had accepted. To prove it to everyone, he proudly held up her left hand which showed a beautiful sapphire ring. She blushed like a young miss.

Expecting the announcement to be made, William had ordered bottles of champagne readied. With a nod at Filbert, the butler arranged for the bottles to be brought to the drawing room where the family had gathered in preparation for dinner.

"'Tis a fine lass ye have there, Franklin," Mr. Mackay said. "She took verra good care of me when I was laying in me sickbed hearing the rattling of the Grim Reaper." He lifted his glass of champagne and said, "*Slàinte!*"

Aunt Margaret leaned toward Amy's ear. "I don't know what that term means, but it sounds good."

"Perhaps when your husband returns from Scotland, he'll be speaking to you with all those expressions."

"Mayhap. That's Scottish, isn't it?"

"Hmm. I'm not sure."

Aunt Margaret placed her champagne glass on the table

near the window. "What I cannot comprehend is my brother marrying. The man is fifty-five years. Fifteen or so years after your mother's death, he decides to marry?"

Amy looked over at Papa, absolutely glowing. "I don't think his marriage to my mother was a very happy one. I mean, they lived apart all the years of my life."

Aunt Margaret nodded. "That's true. They got along well enough to have two children, but aside from that, being an arranged match, they each went their own ways once you and Michael were born."

"I'm so glad I didn't succumb to Papa's grumbling about me not marrying sooner than I did. I was so grateful when he allowed me to escape London and all its balls and strolls in the park and return to Bath."

Aunt Margaret smiled at her. "Now you have a happy marriage and a beautiful son."

"And you managed to avoid Papa's attempts at getting you married off, too," Amy added.

Her aunt sniffed. "Lord Exeter was *my* choice, and I am quite happy with him."

"And the baby?" Amy asked.

To her surprise, Aunt Margaret smiled. In fact, Amy thought she glowed. "I am getting used to the idea. Charles has helped. Although I don't know that I would ever want to become familiar with nappy changes."

"Ah. Neither do I," Amy said and laughed.

Mrs. Elliot walked over to where Amy and Aunt Margaret stood, her demeanor a bit reticent. "I would like to know your feelings on Franklin and me marrying."

"I think it's wonderful!" Aunt Margaret said.

Amy placed her hand on Mrs. Elliot's arm. "And I as well. What I'm thinking of is when my mother-in-law married Edward. My husband had a hard time accepting that a man found his mother attractive and desirable. Although he never said anything to his mother or Edward, it took him quite a while to be comfortable with it. But I don't have any problem with Papa marrying again."

"Lady Lily and Edward are so very well matched," Mrs. Elliot said. "If you hadn't told me, I would have thought they'd been married for years."

Filbert entered the drawing room. "Dinner is served, my lord, my lady."

The group wandered to the dining room. Their ever-increasing group: Amy, William, Edward, Lady Lily, Aunt Margaret, Papa, Mrs. Elliot, Mr. Mackay, and Mr. Wheeler.

LADY LILY HAD ANNOUNCED at dinner on Wednesday that she had set the opening of the bookstore for Friday. Amy, Aunt Margaret, Eloise, Mrs. Elliot, and Miss Harper worked with Lady Lily and Edward all day Thursday.

The banner Mrs. Elliot had made was perfect. The material was a light blue linen with dark blue stitching announcing the new name of the store: *The Book Nook*. Edward had arranged for the name to be painted on the front of the store, but for the first week or so, they would leave the banner up to capture attention.

Papa stopped in and whisked Mrs. Elliot away for luncheon at the Inn.

It had been a busy day and informative as well. Amy wandered off from the store in the early afternoon and went to the blacksmith. Mr. Morris was busy putting together a very old musket when she entered.

"Good afternoon, Mr. Morris." She nodded at the parts of the gun scattered on the workbench. "That looks like quite an antiquated firearm you have there."

He looked up and pushed his spectacles farther up his nose.

"And good day to you, my lady. This certainly is an old one and sold to me by an almost-as-old-gentleman who was here last week and wanted to get rid of it." He grinned. "I couldn't resist."

"I can understand why. It is very interesting."

"How can I help you, my lady?"

"I just wanted to ask you a question. When Lord Wethington and I were here a couple of weeks ago, you mentioned that Miss Harper had brought in a gun to sell to you."

He moved away from the workbench with parts of guns on it. He rubbed his hands with a soft cloth and studied her. "I think I remember who you are referring to. I didn't know her name. Seemed like a nice girl, however."

"Yes. She is. She's working for my mother-in-law, Lady Lily, since she and her husband, Mr. Colbert, have purchased the bookstore."

"How nice for them. I'm sure the village will be happy to welcome them as new shop owners."

Wanting to get back to the subject she was seeking information about, she said, "I'm curious as to how to sell guns to you. What is involved? Are there ownership documents you need?"

"I only buy the old and unusual guns for my collection. Do you have one to sell?"

"Perhaps. What sort of information did you receive from Miss Harper to buy her gun?"

He shook his head. "I didn't buy her gun. It was a common everyday pistol. I don't buy those."

How interesting. "I see. Well, let me speak with my husband and determine if he does have one to sell."

Mr. Morris looked at her strangely, which made perfect sense since this was truly an odd conversation and the last time they were here William had indicated he might be interested in buying something from Morris's assemblage. "Yes. Well, if it's from his collection I might be interested."

"Have a nice day, Mr. Morris. Be sure to stop into the new bookstore tomorrow for the opening. We will have treats."

"Thank you. Yes, I may do that."

She backed away from the counter. "Thank you for your time." She opened the door and hurried out.

On the way back to the bookstore, she contemplated what Mr. Morris had told her. Miss Harper had been unable to sell her gun. That meant she had the gun when both men were shot. But whatever could be her motive for killing Mr. Reynolds? Of course, that was a moot point since the man was able to bring out the worst in just about everyone he had dealt with.

When she returned to the bookstore, it appeared that everything was ready for the opening the next day. Amy walked up to Miss Harper who was folding napkins to be used in the tearoom area. "I am so happy that Lady Lily hired you."

"Thank you. I am, too. She is such a lovely lady. You are fortunate to have her for a mother-in-law." She blinked rapidly and turned her face so Amy couldn't see her.

She would have to be senseless to not know that the woman was hiding tears.

"Perhaps one day we can have tea together," Amy said, giving the woman time to compose herself. She waved her arm around. "Not here, things will be—one hopes—much too busy. But up at the Manor. What days are you free from your duties here?"

"Tuesday afternoons and Sunday all day because we are closed."

"Well, then, it's settled. You must come for tea on Tuesday. There are several of us planning the Harvest Festival for the village, and we can always use another hand. Although the tea will be just the two of us," she quickly stated, not wanting the girl to change her mind, not knowing many women in the village.

Miss Harper sniffed. "Yes. Thank you, my lady. You are most kind."

* * *

UNFORTUNATELY, the day of the bookstore opening was cloudy and cool, with the threat of rain. However, that did not deter his mother and stepfather from their delight in the endeavor they had worked so diligently on.

William still could not believe that his mother—his mother! —raised as a Lady, the daughter of an earl, married to his father, a viscount from a very old family, was now a store merchant.

But just as marriage to Edward Colbert had changed her somewhat, so did owning a bookstore. In all the years he had known her—all his life—he had never seen her happier. He wondered what his sister, the Countess Denby, currently residing with her husband and children in France, would think of their mother's new life.

Once he finished his breakfast, William wiped his mouth on a napkin and turned to Amy. "I would like some of your time when you are through before you leave for the store."

She nodded and turned toward Lady Margaret who asked her a question.

He headed to the library to await his wife. Once again, he looked at the missive he had received from the bishop, requesting he attend him.

In a matter of minutes, he looked up as Amy entered the room. She walked to the chair in front of the desk and sat.

"I received a missive this morning from Bishop Hughes. He would like me to visit with him Tuesday." He looked up at her. "This is the first contact I've had from him since I notified him of Mr. Smythe's death. I wonder if this has something to do with that?"

"It has taken him long enough. I would like to go with you, but I have invited Miss Harper for tea Tuesday afternoon. Now that we know she still possessed her gun when Mr. Reynolds was murdered, I think it's wise for me to speak with her. Especially with her working for your parents."

William placed his elbow on the desk and rested his chin on his hand. "What connection, if any, did she have with Mr. Reynolds?"

"That I am hoping to find out." She shifted in her chair. "Did we ever gather any more information on Mr. Fletcher? It seems we have forgotten about him."

"You will be happy to know Mr. Wheeler has obtained information on Mr. Reynolds, though."

Amy moved to the edge of her chair. "Indeed? You mean he has done his job?"

William smiled. "Yes. He filed a report with me just yesterday."

"Don't tease me, husband. What did Mr. Wheeler learn?"

"That Mr. Reynolds was disliked by most people in the village, and therefore anyone could have killed him."

Amy sat with her mouth agape. "Truly? That's what he said?"

"Yes, my dear wife. That is what he said. Then he stood there and smugly said, 'I will now work on the vicar's murder.'"

Amy dropped her head in her hands. She looked up and covered her mouth with her hand. "Would you believe me, Husband, if I said I would prefer to have Detectives Carson and Marsh right now?"

"Sad, isn't it?"

She sighed. "If the constable had nothing further to report on, then I am on my way. As you know, the bookstore opening is today, and your parents are very excited. She has sent for a number of my books, and I am to sign them. Providing, of course, that someone buys one," she said with a laugh.

"If no one buys them, my darling, I shall buy them all."

She walked around the desk and kissed the top of his head. "You are very sweet."

He looked up at her. "Do not tell anyone that."

With a bright smile, she left the room.

William sat for a while, contemplating the two murders and their suspects thus far. They needed more information on Mr. Fletcher. Why was he listed in the vicar's appointment book every week, same day, same time? If it was something as innocuous as playing chess, why break into his office to steal the folder?

Although they weren't even sure he was the one to break in or if there even was a folder with his name on it. He had also threatened Reynolds the night before he was found shot, which placed him further up on the list.

Next, Miss Harper, who he had dismissed, but now had to reconsider since she had not sold her gun to Mr. Morris. A woman scorned would provide a motive for Mr. Smythe, but Mr. Reynolds? However, Constable Wheeler did make a logical 'report' when he said Reynolds had many enemies in the village.

Mr. Granger, whose wife was supposedly dallying with the vicar, was still on their list. At first, he had found it hard to believe, seeing as how a vicar should be above such things, but given Granger's reaction to them when they'd met him at the Inn, it did seem to make that accusation more likely.

Reynolds might have also been a target for young Joseph Hamilton, if he was afraid the new vicar might take his father-in-law's side on the idea of annulment.

The problem with all these suspects was the only two who seemed to have an actual motive for the vicar were Miss Harper and Mr. Granger. What they'd learned so far, was she had no motive to kill Reynolds and Granger didn't either, unless he'd had a run in with the man that no one had brought to their attention. But William was certain if he surveyed the village, he would find more people than Fletcher had threatened the man.

And of course, the mysterious Mr. Walsh who purchased a house in the village and decided to sell it only weeks later. Then William chided himself. Were they so very far from solving these murders that he was considering someone guilty merely because he bought a house and decided he didn't like it? Or didn't like the village?

He made a mental note to see how close Franklin was to taking title to the house Walsh was selling him. The man might still be in town and a short visit with him, merely asking about what he found about the village that made him decide to move so suddenly would be in order.

With all of that muddling his brain, he stood and left the study, deciding that celebrating his parents' new venture would be the best thing he would do for the day.

21

William walked to the village for the opening of the bookstore since his parents and Amy had taken the carriage. The early morning clouds had moved off, and with the sun now shining brightly, the air was beginning to warm up.

When he crested the small hill before the village, he was quite pleased to see many shoppers in the village and several of them going in and out of the new bookstore.

As he entered the store, his mother greeted him, a bright smile on her face. She waved her arms around. "What do you think, Son? Isn't it glorious."

He bent and kissed her cheek. "Yes, Mother. It is truly glorious. You and Edward have done a wonderful job."

She pointed to the area in the back of the store that had been designated as the tearoom. "Amy is signing books back there."

He nodded and headed in that direction. Three women stood in a line in front of the table where she sat, each clutching one of Amy's books. She spoke to the woman at the table, then bent her head and signed the book, handing it back with a big smile.

William waited while the other two had their books signed and then approached the table. "It appears you are quite successful today."

Amy grinned. "It has been nice. I think I've signed about ten books, which is quite encouraging since the village is not exactly a bustling city like London or Bath."

Miss Harper approached the table where Amy sat. "Excuse me, my lord, my lady." She smiled in Amy's direction. "Your footman, Carter, I believe his name is, has arrived with the baked goods your cook has sent. Lady Lily and Mr. Colbert are both busy with customers. Where shall we put them?"

Amy stood. "I will show you where they should go." As Amy led the young girl off to collect the treats, William wandered to the shelves and began to browse the books.

"Good morning, my lord. It is a pleasant day, is it not?"

William turned to see the vicar, Mr. Hopkins, standing behind him. "Good morning, Vicar. Yes, it is indeed a pleasant day."

"I understand it is your charming parents who bought the bookstore from one of the villagers who has moved to Brighton."

"Yes. Mrs. Barnes was the previous owner. Her son and his family live in Brighton, and she wanted to join them there. She had owned the store for many years." He slid the book he was holding back onto the shelf. "How are you finding Wething-ford, Mr. Hopkins?"

"I am thrilled to be here. It is a much smaller congregation than what I had in my last church in Carlisle. We had a much larger number of worshippers there."

"We are small but having lived here all the years of growing up, I was always impressed with how devoted so many are to the church."

He smiled softly. "That is very good to know." He looked around the room for a minute. "Do you know where the religious books are shelved? I need some inspiration for my next sermon."

"My parents are using the Dewey Decimal system. If you look on the sign over there against the wall, you will see a listing of where each category is shelved."

Mr. Hopkins patted him on the shoulder. "Thank you so much, my lord. I look forward to seeing you Sunday."

The man wandered off, spent but a few minutes studying the chart on the wall, then left the store. William shook his head. The poor man seemed to be a tad befuddled at times.

"Wasn't that Mr. Hopkins who just left the store?" Amy stood alongside him, looking at the door.

"Yes. He said he was here to find a book for inspiration for his sermon on Sunday. I would think a vicar would have all those books at hand. Especially when he said he had a much larger congregation when he served in Carlisle."

"Carlisle? Is that what he said?"

"Yes. Why?"

Amy tapped her fingertip against her lips. "I am almost certain he said his last church was in North Berwick."

William stared at her for a moment. "I believe you are correct. I was thinking the man seemed a bit muddle-headed when I spoke with him just now. I do hope we won't have to switch vicars again so soon."

"I am certain he is trying his best to adjust to a new place and there will be occasions when he forgets a few things. Or gets them mixed up. I do remember him saying he served in so many places that they all ran together after a while. I just hope he doesn't end up living with us, he and Mr. Mackay sipping brandy in the library and discussing books."

"Enough about the vicar. I see a man standing next to the

table where you are supposed to be signing books, Lady Author."

* * *

"My lady, Miss Harper has arrived." Filbert stood in the doorway with Miss Harper standing behind him. With Amy's nod, he stepped aside, and the woman entered her solar.

She went to stand and then remembered all the 'do and do nots' she had learned with her finishing tutor when she'd gone to London to have her Season.

The rule was a member of the nobility didn't stand for a commoner. How very rude that seemed, so Amy rose to her feet. "Good afternoon, Miss Harper, I am so glad you joined me." She gestured to the settee across from where she had been sitting, working on some disastrous excuse for a needlepoint.

"How do you like your tea?" Amy asked.

"Two sugars and a bit of cream," Miss Harper said.

Once tea had been fixed and plates of small sandwiches and lemon tarts in front of them, Amy said, "How are things going at the bookstore?"

"Just wonderful, my lady. Lady Lily and Mr. Colbert are the best of employers. I am so happy to be there."

"Are you settling in well?" Amy took a sip of tea, hoping her question would not have the poor girl bursting into tears.

Miss Harper placed her cup into the saucer and sighed. "As I told you before, I came to see my betrothed, but once I spoke with him, he informed me that he no longer wished to marry me." She shrugged.

"Oh, I am so sorry. That must have been very painful."

She nodded. "It was." Raising her chin, she continued, "I did what I needed to do to get past it."

Well, then. Whatever did that mean?

"I am hoping the job is helping you move on."

"Yes." She reached for a lemon tart and took a bite.

Amy was at a loss for words. How did one ask one's guest if what she meant by doing what was needed to get past her heartbreak was shooting her betrothed?"

She cleared her throat. "Do you see him often? I imagine that might be painful."

Miss Harper shook her head. "No. He no longer lives here."

Hmm. Is he living underground? Buried in the church graveyard by chance?

"So, tell me about yourself. Where did you live before here?"

"London. My parents passed away when I was young. I spent most of my years in an orphanage." She picked up a crumb from her lap. "When I was too old to stay there, I found a small flat with a reasonable rent—although the section of London was not very nice—and was hired by a woman who owned a millinery shop."

"Is that how you met your betrothed?"

"No." She took a sip of tea. "I understand from your mother-in-law that you have a young son."

Apparently, Miss Harper did not want to speak of her betrothed which was completely understandable. To leave her home in London and travel all the way out to the country only to find rejection was very upsetting, especially for a young girl who had no family to fall back on. It did rather diminish her opinion of Mr. Smythe.

"Yes, he is almost one year old. His formal name is The Honorable Charles George Tottenham, but to us he is merely Charles. He is the most agreeable babe. Presently, he is taking his nap, or I would abscond him from the nursery and have him join us for tea." Amy held up the teapot. "Would you care for more tea?"

"No, thank you, my lady. That was very refreshing."

"Have you found comfortable lodgings here in Wethingford?"

"Now that I have employment, I plan to move into a lovely little cottage near the end of the village once I save enough money. The man who owns it is holding it for me."

"Where are you staying now?"

Miss Harper shrugged. "Oh, here and there."

Uh oh. William would probably throttle her. "If you have nowhere to stay until you can move into your cottage, please consider staying with us."

Miss Harper turned a bright shade of red and shook her head vigorously. "Oh, no, my lady. I could never impose on you that way."

Amy waved her hand in the air. "Oh, I assure you, Miss Harper, you will be one of many who are staying here right now. It would be easy to accommodate one more."

She continued to shake her head. "No. I could not do that."

* * *

"IT WILL ONLY BE for a few days, William. The poor girl has been living on the streets of Wethingford."

"Amy, for heaven's sake. How many people are we going to take in? I'm sure we have more guests than the Inn does. We are competing with them."

She folded her arms across her chest and glared at him. "She is a young, broken-hearted girl, with no family, nowhere to go, and has just now started a job. At your parents' store."

William ran his fingers through his hair. "You do realize she is still on our list of suspects? All you know of Miss Harper is that she possesses a gun, claimed to be betrothed to our vicar who was murdered with a gun, and says she has no family because she was raised in an orphanage."

"Are you suggesting she lied to me?"

He threw his hands up. "I don't know what I'm suggesting.

But I have a feeling you have already planned for her to move in."

Amy made a circle on the corner of his desk with her fingertip. "Well, yes." She straightened and looked him in the eye. "This is my home, too."

"Yes, indeed it is." He began to count on his fingers. "And it is also home to my parents, your father, his betrothed, your aunt, Mr. Mackay, Mr. Wheeler, and now Miss Harper. Have I left anyone out?"

Amy narrowed her eyes at him. "I don't think I care for your attitude."

"My goodness, children. Whatever is going on in here? You can be heard all the way to the village." William's mother entered the library where the 'discussion' was going on between Amy and him.

"My apologies, Mother. I didn't realize we were getting that loud."

She patted him on the cheek like he was ten years. "Fortunately, I was the only one downstairs. The rest are all dressing for dinner." She looked back and forth between the two of them. "Which appears to be what you both need to do."

William waved at Amy who proceeded him out the door, up the stairs, and into their bedchamber.

He turned to her, his hands on his hips. "I know you will not let this go until Miss Harper is safe and snug in her room near the rest of the 'guests'."

"Um, she is already here. When I left her, she was in the nursery playing with Charles."

"You let a suspect in two murders play with our child?"

"Oh, please, William. I am quite sure we can remove her from our list of suspects. She has no connection to Mr. Reynolds—"

"That you know of. Did you ask her if she brought her gun

along with her? Or do we check our guests at the door for weapons now?"

Amy sat on the bed, her head in her hands. "I am weary, William. I do not want to argue with you. I only thought I would help the poor girl out."

He sat alongside her on the bed and put his arm around her shoulders. "I know. You are merely too softhearted."

He reached over and smoothed the hair from her forehead that had fallen from her topknot, then kissed her wrinkled brow. "Do not fret. If you trust the girl and Mother trusted her enough to hire her for the store, then I bow to my females."

Amy rested her head on his shoulder. "I don't know what is wrong with me lately. My stomach still troubles me, I am fatigued all the time and prone to weeping."

"You are doing too much. Even though we have a staff of servants to clean and feed us, you are busy with your writing, keeping up with Charles, helping at the bookstore, and trying to solve two murders. I suggest you take a break from it all."

She raised her head and looked at him. "What happened with your meeting with the bishop?"

"He sent a missive that he had something urgent come up, and we are to meet now next week. He will send another message when he has a specific day in mind."

"I doubt he will want to speak with you on Sunday, which is the day of the Harvest Festival, and we really need you here for that. As Lord of the Manor"— she grinned—"you must judge many of the contests."

"Oh, no, please. How does one do that without hurting anyone's feelings?"

"I have arranged so that the contests you judge will have no names on the entries. That way no one can say you favored one person over another."

"What sort of contests are we talking about, so I can be prepared?"

Amy counted on her fingers. "The livestock will be judged by Mr. Jackson, the stonemason. You will be needed to judge the needlework entries and the baking offerings. Then there are the jams and the quilts."

He groaned and stood and began to change for dinner.

"That reminds me, I need to speak with Mr. Hopkins to make sure he is prepared to lead the prayers of thanksgiving at the church before the Festival begins." Amy turned so William could unfasten her gown.

He whipped the cords loose. "I suggest you do that soon. The man is confused at best and incompetent at worst. In fact, when I meet with the bishop, I will try to be kind, but find out exactly how this man has been a vicar for years and reads the wedding ceremony instead of the graveside prayers."

"Yes, William, be kind. He is a man of the cloth."

Once finished with their grooming, they headed to the drawing room to await dinner.

Lady Margaret broke from the crowd and hurried across the room, parts of her hairdo falling onto her shoulder. "I bought a new pet to replace Othello!"

"How exciting," Amy said. "What did you get?"

She held up a furry animal. "A sweet little kitten."

William took one look at the bundle of fur in her arms and sneezed.

22

"*I*'m so excited that the mystery book club has been revived," Amy said as she and William left the house and entered the carriage. "And I think the new tearoom at the bookstore is the perfect place for it."

He settled in the seat across from her. "I agree, however, I believe no one is as excited as Edward. Not only does he get to run the meetings again, but he owns the store where the club meets. I know many of the members browse and buy books before and after the meetings."

Amy shook her head. "Your mother in business."

"I know. She's like an entirely different person than the woman who raised me. She was such a stickler for doing everything the correct way. Who one could and could not associate with, and what one could and could not do."

"Then she moved from London, met Edward and married, and they now live in the country and own a bookstore."

"Speaking of my mother marrying after years of widow-hood, how do you feel about your father marrying after so many years?"

Amy tapped her lips with her fingertip. "I know you were a

bit uncomfortable with Edward seeing your mother in a way that—"

"Stop right there."

Amy laughed. "William, your mother is a person, a woman."

He tugged at his neckcloth. "I know precisely what she is. She is my mother. She never engages in the activities to which you were about to refer."

She laughed harder. "William, how do you think she birthed you and your sister?"

"Immaculate conception." At least he grinned.

"If that is what you wish to believe, I will not dissuade you. As far as my papa getting married again, I think it is a good thing. I already see Mrs. Elliot brings out a softer side of him. It is important for everyone to be happy in their lives, and I don't think Papa was particularly happy for a long time."

"Very generous of you, dear wife."

She shrugged. "I have nothing to lose. Perhaps the fact that I saw him so little growing up has something to do with me not feeling as you do. I am sure he took care of his needs—"

William held up his hand. "Stop please. Us conversing about our parents' private life is making me itchy."

Her brows rose. "Hmm. Considering how active our own 'private life' is, I would not think of you as a prude."

He raised his chin and looked down at her. "I am not a prude. And I wish this conversation to be finished." He looked out the carriage window. "We are here anyway."

He assisted a still laughing Amy out of the carriage.

"Children, I am so happy you arrived early." Lady Lily hurried up to them, concern on her face.

"What is wrong, Mother?"

She looked at Amy. "When your father and Mrs. Elliot stopped by the vicarage earlier today to make plans for their wedding, they mentioned the book club and the vicar told them he would be delighted to join us." She stopped to take a deep breath.

"And?"

Edward walked up and placed his hand on Lady Lily's shoulder. "Your mother is concerned that the book we have chosen for this week is much too," he looked at his wife, "what was the word you used?"

"Improper for a vicar to be expected to read and comment on."

"Mother, surely you haven't selected something inappropriate?"

Edward shook his head. "Not at all. We decided on *Murders in the Rue Morgue.*"

"Edgar Allen Poe," Amy said.

"I don't see a problem with it, Mother."

"He might think it's too…unworthy of a vicar to read."

Edward smiled. "Your mother seems to think the vicar is equivalent to one of the saints."

Amy hugged her mother-in-law. "I think you are concerned over nothing. None of us knows the vicar very well, but I don't see him as overly pious. And I do hope we will not choose books to read because the vicar is a member."

Just then a few of the book club members entered. "The store is just lovely, Lady Lily. You and Mr. Colbert have done a wonderful job," Mrs. Applegate said as she looked around the area. As always, she was well-dressed with a hat that Amy had to look away from, lest she laugh. The size was tremendous, and there were several birds atop it, along with netting and ribbons.

"Since we have arrived early, I plan to browse the bookshelves," Mrs. Applegate said as she removed her gloves.

"I shall do the same," Miss Martin said.

Within minutes, the rest of the book club members arrived.

A few who had been involved when Mrs. Barnes had owned the store, and a couple of new ones.

Edward stood at the front of the tearoom. "Please find seats when you are ready. We expect to begin the meeting in about ten minutes."

Amy was pleased to see such a fine turnout. She looked around the room at Mrs. Applegate, Miss Martin, Mr. Moore, Mr. Graves, Mrs. Armstrong, and Miss Harper.

Amy approached Miss Harper who was looking better every day. It appeared she was recovering from her broken betrothal. "It is so nice of you to join us, Miss Harper, considering you spend so much of your time here."

"I just love this store, my lady. Lady Lily is such a fine employer and allows me time to browse the bookshelves when the store is quiet and all the dusting and other chores are finished."

Mrs. Applegate summoned her, so Amy left Miss Harper.

The members exchanged pleasantries, a few of them browsing the bookshelves. Others chatted while fixing a cup of tea from the table Lady Lily had set out with refreshments.

The meeting was just about to begin when Mr. Hopkins entered. "Good evening, everyone. It is a pleasure to see so many villagers interested in reading."

"Good evening to you, Mr. Hopkins. Please take a seat. We were just about to start."

Mr. Graves stood. "Take my seat, vicar."

Once they were both settled, Edward said, "Since this is our first night gathering as a new group, we don't have an assigned book to discuss, but I think it would be of interest to the group tonight if we held a discourse on books that we've already read.

"For this coming week, we will be reading *The Murders in the Rue Morgue* and then holding an analysis of it next week. After that, we will take suggestions from the group and vote to decide on a book to read."

"*Murders in the Rue Morgue.* Such a mystifying story," Mr. Hopkins said.

Edward addressed him. "Since we are a mystery book club, we do select mystery books. On occasion we might delve into something else, but for the most part, we choose mysteries."

Mrs. Applegate turned to face Mr. Hopkins. "Vicar, are you aware that Lady Wethington is our local famous author?"

He looked over at her. "No, I did not know that. What sort of books do you write, my lady?"

"Murder mystery," Lady Lily said before Amy could answer.

The vicar's brows rose. "Indeed? Such an odd subject for a young lady. Have you published any books? I don't seem to remember seeing your name on the bookshelves."

William laughed. "That is because she writes under E. D. Burton."

Obviously surprised, he said, "I know that author. In fact, I am sure I've read a book or two of yours, Lady Wethington." He dipped his head. "I am impressed. Has the group ever read any of your books?"

"The book club his lordship and I belonged to in Bath read most, if not all, of my books. I think some of the members here have read them."

"Indeed, my lady. I just bought another one the day of the bookstore opening, and you were nice enough to sign for me," Miss Martin said.

Mr. Graves nodded. "Myself as well."

Mr. Hopkins nodded at the group. "It seems you are quite popular, Lady Wethington. I must peruse my bookshelves at home and have you sign the books I already own."

Edward cleared his throat as a signal for the meeting to begin.

* * *

Following the Sunday church service, the much-anticipated Harvest Festival began. Mr. Hopkins had given a brief sermon, stating he knew everyone was anxious to begin the Festival, and he didn't wish to cause trouble for the parents of the little ones who were fidgeting in their seats.

The congregants hurried from the building, giving veracity to the vicar's statement. Eager children hopped up and down, and parents smiled at their enthusiasm as the group spread out to enjoy the day.

William approached the table full of baked goods that he was to taste and select a winner. He pulled Amy close. "My dear, I wish you had not sacrificed me for this duty."

She looked up at him, her hand over her eyes, blocking the bright sun. "I didn't. Apparently, it is the job of the Lord of the Manor to pick the winners of several of the events."

While he was stuck doing this difficult endeavor, the men had gathered for a horseshoe tossing contest. To some cheering and some moaning, Mr. Jackson, the stonemason, had bested the first of his challengers. Many a young lady cast her eyes in his direction.

"I believe I will take a walk around while you get yourself into trouble, Husband," Amy said as she grinned and left him to pick winners.

He sighed and accepted the spoon from Miss Martin who gazed longingly at what must have been her offering. There was a contest for sweet baked goods, jams and jellies, needlepoint, and quilting. He knew nothing of the last two and hoped Amy would return before he got to those entries.

"My lord, I'm sure you will be quite pleased with my short-bread," Mrs. McCabe said, glancing toward a plate next to Miss Martin's dish.

This would certainly not be a fair contest if these ladies each tried to sway him by impetuously pointing out their own dishes.

"Ladies, if you please. I would like this to be a fair contest. Therefore, I shall request a blindfold so I can truly not know which lovely dish I am eating. They all look wonderful, and I know it will be difficult for me to select one."

After a bit of grumbling, he was presented with a linen cloth that he tied around his head.

"Now the judging shall begin."

* * *

AMY WANDERED THE GREEN, admiring tables overflowing with vegetables and fruit being sold, a tribute to the harvest they were celebrating. Other tables sold handcrafted items neatly displayed. She could also smell meat pies and some sort of stewed meat and vegetables.

In her meandering, she was able to speak with Mr. Morris about his gun collection and Mr. Fletcher about his problem with Mr. Reynolds.

"Yes, I had a problem with Reynolds," Mr. Fletcher said when she approached him. "He was always blathering about one thing or another. Most times I ignored what the fool man said because he was always in his cups. He had many a nasty thing to say about the vicar."

"Were you close friends with Mr. Smythe?"

"I could say that. We had a standing appointment each week to play chess. We were well matched, and I must say I really miss that." He shook his head and wandered off toward the Inn.

Mr. Fletcher's statement, of course, while explaining why his name was in the vicar's appointment book every week, only strengthened her idea of Reynolds killing Mr. Smythe, but it was hard to convict a dead man.

Joseph Hamilton and Jane were wandering the tables. She looked much better than the day of the funeral and wore that glow many pregnant women did. After a brief conversation with them, she moved on, trying her best to speak with all the people on their suspect list. The gathering presented a great opportunity.

Next, she approached Mr. Granger looking disconcerted at her. "My lady, I do want to apologize for the way I treated you and his lordship at the Inn a couple of weeks back. I have adjusted to my new situation with my wife living with her mother." He shrugged. "Some things are not meant to be, it seems."

She patted him on the arm. "I am glad you are feeling better."

She made her way back to William more frustrated than ever. Just about everyone on their suspect list was slowly being erased. Someone had to kill the vicar and Mr. Reynolds. Mayhap even two someones.

"My lady, this is a beautiful celebration, is it not?" Mr. Wheeler stepped in front of her, wearing his Constable shirt and grinning.

"Yes, it is indeed a wonderful celebration. I see you are doing constable things: walking around, keeping the peace."

He drew himself up and stuck out his chest. "Indeed I am. I have my eye on everyone."

"Have you obtained any more information on the murders?"

His chest deflated. "No. I am still at sixes and sevens. Since I know so few people, it is hard." He leaned in closer to her ear. "I do have a suspect, but I will not disclose him until I have more information."

"Indeed? Can you not share him with me?"

He shook his head. "No, my lady. Police procedures. I shall continue my investigation and let you and his lordship know as soon as I am certain."

She smiled and wished him a good day. If she thought the man really had a suspect, she would have pressed him, but she doubted he was able to uncover anyone she and William hadn't already considered and then dismissed.

She found William still judging the contests. He looked almost panicked, so she had the feeling it hadn't gone well. She walked up to him. "How are the contests going?"

He whipped the blindfold off and used it to wipe the sweat from his forehead. Yanking her arm, pulling her near him. "You must help me, Wife. Everyone is mad at me, and I still have one more contest to judge."

"Which one is it?"

He waved at one of the tables. "Needlepoint. Now how the blasted hell am I to decide which needlepoint is best?"

"Husband. Calm yourself." She patted him on the arm. "As Lady of the Manor, I shall pick the winner of the needlepoint. You may leave now and go to the Inn for a nice mug of ale. When this is over, I shall join you."

"Amy, dear, have I told you lately that I love you?"

"No. But I know it." She pushed him. "Go."

William strode away, dodging crowds of people shopping, looking, strolling, and otherwise making his escape difficult. It appeared the entire village, along with the outlying county, had decided to celebrate.

Amy turned to the women who stood around the needlepoint display. "I apologize, his lordship has been called away. I shall stand in his stead."

Six women began to talk all at once, waving their arms.

Amy held up her hand. "No, please do not speak. I just want to look at the fine work without knowing—or guessing—who did which piece."

Reluctantly, they closed their mouths and stood back. Amy looked carefully at each one. They were all lovely and something she couldn't ever do. Finally, she picked a pillow with a lovely design of a valley with two mountains behind it. The shading was so wonderful, it almost looked like a painting.

After announcing the winner and buying all the entries with instructions to have them delivered to the Manor, she made her escape to the Inn to join William.

"Where are you racing off to?" Aunt Margaret took her hand and tugged. "I have been searching for you for a while now."

"I've been speaking with the villagers, and just now judged a needlepoint contest and purchased all the entries."

Her aunt smiled at her. "You are so soft-hearted, Amy."

She grimaced. "So I've been told." She linked her arm through her aunt's. "I am on my way to the Inn to meet William for an ale. Would you care to join us?"

"Yes. That sounds lovely."

They had barely seated themselves at William's table when Mr. Hopkins joined them. "Good afternoon, my lord, my lady." He turned to Aunt Margaret. "Good afternoon, Lady Exeter."

"Very good memory, Vicar, considering you've met so many people since your arrival."

"Ah, yes. It is one of the skills vicars must possess."

"Would you care to join us for a mug of ale?" William asked as he waved to one of the chairs.

The vicar pulled out a chair and sat. "I think a mug of ale is quite nice right now."

23

One thing Amy had never expected to do was dress for her papa's wedding. Yet that was what she and William were doing in their bedchamber.

It was also a remarkable day because William would leave for Reading for his meeting with the bishop after the wedding celebration. Lady Lily and Edward would be taking up residence in their own house. With the book club meeting that evening, they had moved all their belongings the day before.

This afternoon, Miss Harper would be moving into her cottage, and Mr. Wheeler had secured a flat in the village.

Once Papa and Mrs. Elliot—who would not be Mrs. Elliot after the wedding—returned from their wedding trip, they would move into the house Papa had purchased from Mr. Walsh. Mrs. Elliot explained that Mr. Walsh and his wife had separated, which was why he bought the house in Wethingford. But they had reconciled and were returning to their home in Bristol.

The Manor would be so very quiet with only her, Aunt Margaret, and Mr. Mackay in residence once William departed. After all the noise and chaos of the past few weeks, she wasn't sure if she looked forward to the silence or felt a tad lost. But at least she would be able to spend time on her writing and coming up with more suspects for the two real murders.

Never had they been at such loose ends with murder investigations. Was it because these two were in a small village? Or because they didn't have Carson and Marsh stumbling in front of them? Actually, the detectives were usually a few steps behind them. However, William had promised to help her continue with the search upon his return.

A slight knock on the bedchamber door drew her attention. "Yes?"

"Amy, it is me," Aunt Margaret said. "Are you two ready? I believe Franklin is growing nervous."

"Yes. We shall be right down." She turned her back to William. "Can you fasten me up, please?"

With practiced ease, her husband had her gown done up within seconds.

"Do you have matching shoes?" he asked as he looked in the mirror, fixing his ascot.

"Yes, and they even match my gown."

He grinned at her through the mirror. "Good job, Lady Wethington."

She retrieved her gloves and reticule and stood before him. "I am ready."

He studied her for a minute, then reached out and adjusted her hat. "Now we are ready."

Papa stood at the entrance, speaking with Edward. He looked up as they descended the stairs. "It's about time, Daughter. We must leave for the church."

"We have plenty of time, Papa. You are just anxious."

Mrs. Elliot had spent the night with her friend, Mrs. Peters, and would meet them at church. "Have the others left for church?"

"Yes. We must hurry," Papa said.

The six of them climbed into Papa's carriage, a tad bigger than William's, with more room for them. The others had taken William's carriage earlier.

It was a pleasant day, quite rare for October. With the threat of winter weather soon, Papa had arranged for him and his new wife to travel to Italy for warmer temperatures.

Everything was ready for the celebration following the ceremony. Thankfully, Amy was able to leave the wedding breakfast in the capable hands of Mrs. O'Sullivan and Cook.

William leaned over toward Amy. "Let us hope the vicar doesn't read the interment prayers."

Amy laughed. "Yes. I certainly hope so."

Many of the villagers were in the church since Mrs. Elliot had lived in the village all her life. The bride herself stood at the back of the church, dressed in a lovely pale blue gown. She carried a bouquet of flowers and looked truly radiant.

When Amy smiled at her, she suddenly realized she was gaining a stepmother. How very odd that sounded. Mrs. Elliot had said her daughter was unable to attend the wedding because she recently discovered she was in a family way and her husband did not want her to travel. Apparently, Papa had promised her they would visit her daughter when the weather was warmer.

That also reminded her she was gaining a stepsister.

Well, then.

She'd spent her entire life with just one brother. Now she was anxious to meet Mrs. Elliot's daughter—her stepsister. She hadn't known her before they approached Mrs. Elliot for the job of taking care of Mr. Mackay.

So many changes taking place this day.

William took her arm and led her up the aisle to the front pew to join Eloise, Lady Lily, and Edward. Mr. Mackay, Miss Harper, and Mr. Wheeler sat behind them.

Papa and Michael walked to the front of the church from

CALLIE HUTTON

the side entrance, Michael acting as his groomsman. The music started up, and Mrs. Elliot walked down the aisle, preceded by Aunt Margaret who was her attendant. Amy glanced between Mrs. Elliot and Papa and would never forget the look on his face. She felt foolish when a tear slid down her cheek.

Mr. Hopkins smiled at the bride and groom, then looked down at his book. "Dearly beloved, we are gathered today to join this man and this woman in holy matrimony."

William smiled at her. "Well, at least he is reading the correct passage."

"A relief."

The service was short, as most of Mr. Hopkins' were, and soon they were all outside the church, kissing cheeks and shaking hands. Amy made it a point to speak with every villager who attended and invited them to the wedding breakfast. She'd already warned Mrs. O'Sullivan to expect more guests than they had planned on.

The wind had picked up while they were in church, so the attendees quickly made their way to the Manor.

The guests all chatted away as they gathered in the drawing room to allow the staff time to set up the dining room to accommodate the additional guests. Amy had always felt a bit silly eating in the formal dining room that was so very large with an immense table. Today, however, she was grateful for it.

William had champagne delivered to the kitchen earlier and now the footmen walked the room with trays of the drink.

Papa had his arm around Mrs. Elliot's waist—rather Anne, as she had asked Amy to call her—as he drank the champagne, gazing at his new wife from time to time.

After about a half hour, they were summoned to the dining room. The breakfast was wonderful, with eggs and bacon, kidneys, cold meats, and kippers and kedgeree. Fresh rolls and bread were offered by the footmen as they approached each guest.

A small table by the doorway held a beautiful wedding cake.

It was a lively gathering with the villagers easily conversing with the family members. Mr. Mackay, who sat across from Amy, stood and offered a Scottish wedding blessing.

Three times.

After a few hours of celebrating, the guests began to leave. Amy made a trip to the kitchen to thank Cook for an outstanding meal and then stopped by Mrs. O'Sullivan's small office behind her bedroom and thanked her as well. William had already offered his thanks to Filbert to pass along to the footmen.

With those duties finished and the last of the guests gone, William and Amy retired to the library. "When are you leaving for Reading?"

"I have a ticket for the 4 o'clock train. I'll have Benson drive me to the station so you will have the carriage for your use while I am gone."

"I thought about going with you this time since I was unable to on the original date, but I think I will use the quiet time to get more of my writing finished and play with Charles, take him to the village. I feel as though with everything going on, I've been neglecting him."

"Ah, yes. I believe it is called mother's guilt."

They were both silent for a minute, then William said. "It was quite nice, actually, to have a wedding where no one was murdered." Referring to their wedding where her cousin was poisoned, Amy nodded. "Yes. The entire wedding breakfast as well as the ceremony in the church was very nice. Mrs. Elliot—sorry I keep forgetting she is now Lady Winchester, or as she asked me to call her, Anne—told me she was very happy with the wedding breakfast. She hugged me and called me 'daughter.'"

"I noticed Mr. Hopkins enjoyed the champagne," William said with a smirk.

Amy laughed. "Yes, but I imagine a vicar does not have the funds to purchase such things."

She shifted on her seat. "It only occurred to me today that I now have a stepmother. And a stepsister."

"Yes. You must get used to it as I had to when I gained a stepfather upon my mother's marriage."

They remained quiet for a few minutes, each taken up with their own thoughts. Then William said, "They are off now on their trip?"

Amy stretched out and removed her shoes. They had been pinching her toes for a while. "Yes. Papa had train tickets for Paddington Station where they will begin their trip."

"It will be a quiet house now."

"Truly. Miss Harper is moving out this afternoon, your parents are already gone, Mr. Wheeler is helping Miss Harper move, and then he is settling into his own flat. Once you leave, it will be me, Aunt Margaret, and Mr. Mackay."

"When do you suppose Mr. Mackay will leave?" William asked.

They looked at each other and burst into laughter.

* * *

AMY ENTERED the bookstore and slipped off her gloves. Lady Lily and Edward were speaking with Mrs. Applegate and Mr. Moore. She had her copy of *The Murders at the Rue Morgue* tucked into her reticule and was looking forward to their discussion this evening.

She had taken a nice nap after William had left. She was so very tired after she kissed him goodbye. Perhaps because of the stress of the wedding and the celebration, but she fought back tears with him leaving. Strange, how out of sorts she felt of late.

He wouldn't be gone long. Since he took the afternoon

train, he would see the bishop tomorrow. If that didn't take too long, he would come home tomorrow, but most likely spend the night at a local inn and return Friday.

"Oh Lady Wethington, what a lovely ceremony and wedding breakfast for Mrs. Elliot and your father." Mrs. Applegate covered her mouth with her hand. "Oh, goodness. I guess I must get used to calling her Lady Winchester now that she's married."

Amy patted her hand. "I am sure she will want you to continue to call her Anne. She doesn't appear to be a very formal person."

"Yes, perhaps, but she is married to a marquess now. That puts her out of our social circle."

Amy laughed that the woman did not realize she, herself, was the daughter of a marquess and married to a viscount. "Mrs. Applegate, do not fret."

Mr. Hopkins walked up to them. "Ah, I see the excellent hostess of Wethington Manor has managed to make it to the meeting tonight."

She smiled at the man. "Yes, but with Lord Wethington gone, I treated myself to a nap this afternoon in order to feel refreshed for the meeting."

"Oh? Where is his lordship?"

"Reading. He had an appointment with the bishop."

Mr. Hopkins' brows rose. "Our bishop?"

She nodded. "I don't know what it was about, but I am sure he will speak with you when he returns."

The vicar wandered off, and Miss Martin approached them. "Where is his lordship?"

"He is on a trip to Reading. Only for a day or so."

Edward moved to the front of the tearoom and announced the beginning of the meeting. Smiling at his wife sitting right in front of him, which he'd always done as leader of the book club, he asked, "What is the general consensus of *The Murders in the Rue Morgue?*"

A lively discussion ensued with everyone agreeing it was frightening enough.

"My goodness, Mr. Colbert, I had to check the lock on my door numerous times when I read it," Miss Martin said.

"I want to propose that our next book will be one of my lovely daughter-in-law's books. As you all know, she is quite the talented author of mystery novels." He waved in Amy's direction.

Mr. Graves and Mrs. Waters both heartily agreed that they pick one of Amy's books.

After much discussion on which book to choose, they decided on *The Twisted Staircase*.

Amy was quite pleased and encouraged to get back to writing her current novel.

The meeting ended and after hugs from Edward and Lady Lily, she returned to her carriage for the ride home. The house was unusually quiet, almost eerily so. She nodded to Filbert and wearily climbed the stairs despite her earlier nap. She really must see the village healer to see why she was so tired and weepy lately.

Aunt Margaret must have already retired to her bedchamber because all was quiet. Mr. Mackay was most likely sitting in the library, sipping on brandy, and reading.

Maybe she'd gotten so used to the chaos of her life of late that she felt a tad restless, or as William would say, 'itchy'.

She entered her bedchamber, wishing with all her heart that William was with her, teasing her, making her laugh, adjusting her clothes. Goodness, if this kept up, she would be weeping for no reason.

She shook herself for the nonsense and began to undress when there was a light knock on her bedchamber door. "Yes."

Filbert's voice came through. "My lady, my apologies for

disturbing you, but I forgot to give you a message that came for you right after you left for the book club meeting. Shall I save it for morning?"

"No. I will take it now." She opened the door and thanked him. He bowed and left as she closed the door, looking at the folded note. She placed it on the table next to the door and prepared to remove her clothes, remembering William was not there to help her.

She did not want to send for a maid, so, with some struggles, she managed to remove all her clothes and slip on her nightrail, glancing at the bed with a sigh. She had not slept alone since she and William had married. What a fool she had become!

She climbed into bed and brought the missive with her. Opening the note, she read the unfamiliar handwriting and her stomach cramped.

Mind your own matters. Stop asking questions that do not concern you. Instead of wasting your time, watch your son.

Amy gasped and immediately fled the bedchamber, clutching her nightgown as she raced up the stairs to the nursery. She burst through the door, completely out of breath.

The small light on the chest of drawers that remained lit all night cast a warm glow on Charles' small body, curled up, his legs tucked under him, thrusting his little bottom into the air, his thumb in his mouth. She turned as Mrs. Grover opened the door to her bedchamber next to the nursery, her hands clutched at the neckline of her nightgown.

"My lady, is something wrong?"

Amy picked up the sleeping, warm body of her son. "No, Mrs. Grover. I am sorry to disturb you. It's just that with his lordship gone to Reading, I would prefer to have Charles sleep in my bed."

The nanny looked skeptically at her but nodded. "Yes, my lady. If that is what you prefer."

"Yes." She pulled a blanket from Charles's crib, wrapped it around him, and headed for the door. "Please, return to your bed, we shall be fine."

Mrs. Grover sniffed. "If you are sure, your ladyship. It is not wise to have a child sleep anywhere except his crib."

Amy nodded, clutching his small body to her. "I understand, and I agree, but with his lordship gone..."

Mrs. Grover nodded and watched her leave as if she was absconding with the lad for nefarious purposes.

Amy made her way downstairs and entered her bedchamber, holding fast to Charles. With tears falling, she climbed into bed. "William, please come home. We need you."

She slid down, her arms wrapped around her son's small, warm body, and offered prayers for the safety of her husband and his quick return.

Sleep was not to be her escape that night, but she was grateful that her son slept on, wrapped in his mother's love, unaware of her anxiety.

24

William enjoyed a breakfast of sausages, eggs, tomatoes, beans, buttered bread, and stewed apples before setting out from the Goose and Goblin Inn to his meeting with the bishop. It was ridiculous, he knew, but he'd felt a tad restless since he'd left Amy in Wethingford. Mayhap because it was their first time apart since they'd married, but he could not attribute his tension completely to that. He had to face it—he missed his wife and son. The sooner this meeting was over and he could return to them, the better he would feel.

He decided to walk the mile or so to the bishop's residence rather than take a hackney. It was a cool and cloudy day, and he was thankful for the greatcoat he'd decided to bring with him on this trip.

He couldn't imagine what the bishop wanted, unless he was looking for a report on Mr. Hopkins. Whatever it was, hopefully it wouldn't take long, and despite his earlier plan, he would take the train home today.

The young cleric who welcomed him invited him to sit in a very comfortable room while he waited for the bishop. The church must be doing well since the room was tastefully done in dark mahogany furniture with deep velvet-cushioned chairs.

Gratefully, it didn't take long before the bishop entered the room. William stood. "Good morning, Bishop. It is a pleasure to see you."

The man held out his hand, and he and William shook. "Please have a seat. We can conduct our business here."

Once they were both comfortable in seats in front of a small, brightly lit fire and William had declined the offer of tea, the bishop rested his folded hands on the table.

"The reason I asked for your attendance is because of the confidential nature of our conversation." He paused for a moment. "For a while I have been expecting, and have now received, a very large donation to the Church of St. Agatha. The benefactor has requested to remain anonymous, but stated he lived a good part of his life in Wethingford and felt the church could use an upgrading, as well as the church cemetery and other grounds around the buildings."

William nodded. "I understand and that is certainly good news, but I don't understand why you requested to tell me about this before our vicar."

The bishop offered a slight, paternal smile. "Mr. Smythe is a young man, and I want to make sure he has guidance with the funds; therefore, I would like to make you trustee of the money."

William smiled. "I assume you mean Mr. Hopkins?"

"Who?"

William frowned. "The new vicar who replaced Mr. Smythe."

"Replaced Mr. Smythe? I am not sure what you are talking about."

Perhaps the bishop was getting on in years and was a tad confused. "Mr. Smythe was, unfortunately, murdered, and after

I notified you, Mr. Hopkins was sent to minister to the villagers in Wethingford."

The bishop turned pale, sweat breaking out on his forehead. "Smythe? Dead? Murdered? My lord, I know nothing of what you speak."

* * *

AUNT MARGARET WALKED into Amy's solar, pulling on a pair of gloves. "Amy, I am off to the village. Lady Lily mentioned they'd gotten in a new shipment of books and a few of them were tomes offering advice to new mothers." She looked at Amy with Charles sitting on her lap, and her brows rose. "Whatever is Charles doing in here?"

Not wishing to upset her aunt in her condition, she shrugged. "Oh, no reason. I've been so busy lately with the Festival and wedding I feel the need to spend time with my son."

"Such a good mother you are. I am impressed." She bent and kissed them both on the head and turned toward the door. "I shall return shortly. Unless the milliner catches my eye. Or perhaps the Sundry Store." She grinned and left the room.

Given her aunt's propensity for shopping, she didn't expect to see her until well past afternoon tea.

Amy leaned her cheek on Charles' head. "Oh, my boy, what shall I do to protect you until your papa returns?"

During the long, dark night when she had jumped at every sound, she thought about the note she'd received. It was printed, so she did not recognize the handwriting. She went over and over in her mind all the suspects they'd had so far, certain that the note came from one of the people who killed either the vicar, Reynolds, or both. She'd come to the conclusion that something was missing, that the person they were looking for was not on their list.

She shivered. The mention in the note of Charles was what frightened her the most. She would not let the lad out of her sight until William returned, which she hoped would be soon. Very soon.

* * *

THE BISHOP STUDIED WILLIAM. "Excuse me, my lord but I am discombobulated. I know nothing of Mr. Smythe being murdered, bless his soul. You say you sent correspondence about this to me?" The bishop's voice was very shaky, and William thought the man could use a good shot of brandy.

"Yes. I sent a letter to you and only a few days later Mr. Hopkins arrived, stating he was the replacement sent by you."

The bishop shook his head the entire time William spoke. "No, my lord, I received no notice of poor Mr. Smythe's tragic death. I also know of no vicar named Mr. Hopkins." The man seemed to be having trouble breathing and was turning a ghastly white.

"Are you well, Bishop? Is there something I can do for you? Call someone to help you?"

"My secretary, please. Mr. Beldon. Have him bring some brandy."

"Yes, right away." Once he reached the door, he turned. "Where is your office, bishop?"

"Turn left, then right at the next corridor." He could hardly get the words out. "My office is two doors down."

A very uncomfortable feeling was growing in William's stomach as he made his way to the bishop's office. Something was very wrong in Wethingford. If the bishop had not sent Mr. Hopkins, then who was he and how would he know to say he was the replacement?

Bloody hell, he must have been the one who murdered Mr. Smythe!

This would be a difficult conundrum to unravel, but his main concern now was getting back home. If Amy mentioned to Mr. Hopkins at the book club meeting the night before that he had a meeting with the bishop today, then Hopkins—whoever he was—would know his ruse was up.

He entered the bishop's outer office. "Excuse me, but the bishop would like you to bring brandy to the room where we were meeting." The young man hopped up. "Yes, my lord. Right away, my lord."

William hurried back to the room where he'd left the bishop with the intention of stating he was returning home immediately.

The bishop looked terrible, and he couldn't leave with the condition he was in. At least not until his secretary arrived with the brandy. Hopefully, it was handy and not something he had to search around for.

"I feel I must be off, bishop. Based on what you have told me, I don't like the fact that my wife and son are at the Manor without my protection."

The bishop put his hand up. "Wait, you must tell me more. Has the killer been found for Mr. Smythe's death?"

"Not yet, but I have a very good idea who it is now. That is why I need to get home as quickly as possible."

The secretary entered with the brandy. William reached out when the man held out a glass to him as well as the bishop. He needed this to settle himself.

The bishop downed almost half a glass of the spirits. "Tell me one more thing, my lord. What does this new vicar—did you call him Mr. Hopkins?"

"Yes."

"What does he look like?"

William described Mr. Hopkins as best he could. The bishop seemed much better after having had the brandy. He shook his head. "I believe your Mr. Hopkins is my former secretary, Mr. Wayman. He handled all my correspondence, and there is no doubt that through his duties he learned about the donation and decided to take it for himself." He stopped for a minute, then his eyes grew wide. "That means..."

"Yes. That is why I am returning home right now. Lady Wethington and Mr. Hopkins belong to the same book club. If she mentioned to him last evening at the meeting that I was visiting with you, he would panic, knowing his plan had crumbled."

The bishop nodded. "God speed you, my lord. Please keep me apprised of the situation."

William nodded and left the room, jogging down the corridor, and out the door. He hailed the first hackney he saw and climbed in. "Railway station. Quickly, please." He pulled out the train schedule in his pocket and checked his timepiece. Eleven o'clock. There was a train at eleven thirty that would get him to the station nearest his house by early afternoon.

As the vehicle pulled into traffic, he tapped his finger on his thigh thinking of Amy—and possibly Charles—in danger.

* * *

SECRETED IN HER BEDCHAMBER, the hours dragged on as she paced with Charles, attempted to eat the breakfast and lunch she'd had sent up from the kitchen, checked the great clock in the corner of her solar numerous times, and finally gave up, collapsing onto the settee, feeling drowsy enough to take a nap.

Charles wrapped in her arms; she had just drifted off to sleep when Filbert knocked on the door. "My lady, I am sorry to disturb you, but the vicar has arrived and asked to speak with you."

How odd. She had just seen him the day before at the wedding and then that evening at the book club meeting. She shrugged. "I will meet him in the drawing room. Just give me a minute to freshen up."

Filbert nodded and left.

She looked down at her wrinkled dress from holding Charles all morning. But since she had no intention of letting him out of her sight until her eyes met William's, it didn't make sense to change. She walked to the bed, placed the baby in the middle of the mattress so he wouldn't wander off, then quickly ran a brush through her hair. She gathered the tresses to the back of her head and tied them with a ribbon. Picking up her grinning, drooling son, she left the room.

"Good morning, Vicar." She entered the room and took a seat across from him. "May I send for refreshments?"

He shook his head and smiled. "No, my lady, do not trouble yourself. I was hoping we could take a stroll in your garden while I discuss a sensitive matter with you."

"Oh, yes, I guess that is possible. I do believe it's a tad chilly out there, so let me go back upstairs and get something warmer for my son to wear."

"I can hold the baby while you're gone."

She hesitated and looked at him, and something in his eyes stopped her as a few things jumped to the forefront of her mind.

Mr. Hopkins didn't seem to know the difference between the marriage ceremony and the interment prayers.

He gave very short, very uninspiring sermons and stumbled over the prayers.

He said his last assignment was in North Berwick, then told William it was in Carlisle.

Only a few days ago at the Festival, Mr. Fletcher stated that before he was murdered, Mr. Reynolds had many a nasty thing to say about the vicar. Amy had assumed he meant Mr. Smythe, but perhaps...

Suddenly very, very afraid, she took a deep breath. She

needed to get herself and Charles upstairs and locked behind closed doors in her bedchamber. She made to head to the door. "Thank you, Vicar, but I will just bring him with me."

He stood. "No, my lady. I don't think so."

She gasped at the very frightening-looking gun facing her.

Mr. Hopkins put his arm out. "Hand me the baby."

Her mouth dry as a desert, she shook her head furiously. "No."

"Yes."

With Charles in her arms, she turned her back on him. "You may shoot me, the sound of which will bring my staff running, but you will not get your hands on my son."

"Do not be so dramatic, my lady. I am not going to shoot you in the back, and I am not going to harm your child either."

She looked at him over her shoulder, still sheltering Charles. "I cannot think of any reason why I should believe that."

He waved the gun at her. "Sit. You're giving me a crick in my neck."

Sensing his mother's anxiety, Charles began to fuss. She sat and rubbed his back, but it didn't settle him."

"Make him stop crying."

"He senses I'm nervous, and it's doing the same thing to him."

A knock at the drawing room door drew their attention. The door opened, and Mr. Wheeler entered. "I apologize, my lady, but I returned to fetch a few more of my things." He looked over the vicar. "Oh, good afternoon, Mr. Hopkins."

Amy noticed the gun the vicar had been holding was no longer visible.

Mr. Wheeler strolled into the room and sat alongside Amy. He looked at the baby. "Oh, poor Charles. Is it time for his nap?"

Amy licked her dry lips. "Yes, it is. Would you mind bringing him upstairs to Mrs. Grover in the nursery?"

If the constable found anything odd about her request, he didn't show it. "Of course, my lady. The nursery is on the top floor, correct?"

"Yes." She held her breath while the young man left the room with Charles. Then let the air out of her lungs when the door closed. Now she only had to worry about herself.

"If that bothersome man returns, see that you get rid of him."

She hoped Mr. Wheeler would return. As a constable, he should help in the situation she found herself in.

"I do not understand why you are here, Mr. Hopkins."

He leaned back, his foot resting on his knee, the gun alongside him so it wasn't visible to anyone entering the room, but she could see it clearly. She wondered if she could run fast enough without getting shot, but since this man most likely killed one, and possibly two people with a gun, she didn't want to try it. William could never get along without her.

"I worked as secretary to the bishop. I learned that St. Agatha's was receiving a very large donation. It might be sinful of me, but I think the money would suit me better than the church."

"I still don't understand," she said, listening to see if Mr. Wheeler was returning to the room.

"I got rid of Mr. Smythe—"

"—you mean, you killed him."

He shrugged. "Yes. Then I went back to Reading and continued to work as the bishop's secretary until the letter from your husband arrived, telling the bishop about poor Mr. Smythe's murder. I destroyed the letter, quit my job with the bishop, and presented myself to Wethingford as the new vicar."

"Waiting for the money to come so you could abscond with it."

"You are a very bright woman, Lady Wethington. That is precisely why you are the one I visited. When you said your husband was visiting the bishop today, I knew my game was up. Also, as a murder mystery author, I figured—and apparently rightly so—that you couldn't resist trying to find the culprit."

"And you sent the note last night?"

"Yes, indeed. I followed you for a while at the Harvest Festival, watched as you questioned people like some sort of detective." He shook his head. "Not well done, Lady Wethington. A woman should be busy with her home, husband, and child. Not writing murder mysteries or trying to solve real life ones."

Perhaps if she kept him talking someone would come to her rescue. It was too bad the crowds of people had moved out of her house. "And what about Mr. Reynolds?"

"Ah. Mr. Reynolds. He was a blathering idiot. He recognized me from the gaming hell in London where we both wasted our time. He started talking about it at the Inn one night. I invited him to meet me in the woods so we could come to an agreement suitable for both of us."

"And you killed him, too."

"The man had the nerve to try to blackmail me. Said if I didn't pay him a tremendous amount of money, he would tell Lord Wethington what I was about."

"Why do you want me? Are you going to kill me, too, and just keep doing it until the money arrives?"

"No, my dear. You are not thinking clearly. Your husband is with the bishop as we speak. There is only one way now to get the money."

"And what is that?"

* * *

WILLIAM ARRIVED at the Manor completely out of breath and scared to death. Filbert had the door open before he even left the hackney. Mr. Wheeler stood in the entrance hall. "You are just in time, my lord."

"Why are you here? Where are my wife and child?"

Wheeler placed his hands on his hips. "The lad is safe with his nanny in the nursery with instructions to keep the door locked until either you or I tell her she can leave."

William shook his head. "What the devil is going on?" He turned to Filbert.

The butler looked muddleheaded for the first time William ever remembered.

"I am not sure, my lord. Lady Wethington has been carrying little Charles around all day. Then Mr. Hopkins arrived—"

"He is here!?"

"Yes." He pointed to the drawing room door. "He is in there with Lady Wethington."

William ran his fingers through his hair.

Wheeler stepped in front of the drawing room door, blocking William. "My lord, with the two of us, we can get her out safely, then I shall arrest him."

"Does he have a gun? William said.

"Yes. I saw it, even though he was attempting to hide it when I was in there on the pretext of telling her ladyship that I was picking up a few of my belongings. I had suspected Mr. Hopkins for some time, but I didn't want him to be aware of that. Last evening when he was at the book club meeting, I broke into the vicarage looking for the gun. I could not find it, but there was evidence that he did possess one. I was sure he had it on him."

"What are his plans? To kill all of us? The bishop knows about this now, so there won't be any money coming to the vicarage."

"I have a feeling he plans to hold your wife hostage until money—either from the bishop or you—is brought to him."

William started toward the drawing room door. "I must go in there. I need to see what is happening."

Wheeler pulled him back. "No. I cannot let you do that. You forget I am law enforcement here in the village."

The entire day had been one surprise after another. But for some reason, the look in Wheeler's eyes told him the opinion he'd had of the young man before now was incorrect. And most likely the man had allowed that on purpose.

Wheeler looked at William. "I noticed when I was in the room with Mr. Hopkins and her ladyship that the room has French doors."

"Yes. That is correct."

"Do you know if they are locked?"

William looked at Filbert.

"Yes, my lord. We lock all the doors at nighttime and most likely it is still locked."

"Then we need another plan," Wheeler said. He paced, his fist under his chin, and thought for a minute while William's heart raced. He wanted to burst into the room, grab his wife, and get her the hell out of there. But with the madman inside the room, in possession of a gun and responsible for two murders at his hand, that wasn't the smartest idea.

"You have been away, have you not, my lord?" Wheeler asked.

"Yes. After the wedding yesterday, I left for Reading to see the bishop. That is how I learned about Mr. Hopkins' deception. I then returned as quickly as possible."

"Then this is what we will do. We will rely on confusion. You, my lord, will burst into the room, eager to see your wife after your trip, talking and waving your arms. I will follow right behind you, blocking your wife, telling her ladyship that I now have all my belongings." He turned to Filbert. "You will be next to enter the room and begin speaking, causing even more confusion."

He looked over at William. "You will give your wife a proper hug and with everything else going on, get her out of that room as quickly as possible. Filbert will follow. I will take care of Mr. Hopkins."

William wasn't quite sure this was the best plan of action, but without another idea and the minutes ticking by with Amy in the room, a gun pointed at her, he had to go along.

"All right, are we ready?"

William regarded Filbert who was looking quite green. He slapped him on the back. "Stay strong. Just one more of your duties."

Wheeler took a deep breath. "On the count of three. Let's make this as noisy, chaotic, and confusing as we possibly can."

William opened the door so firmly that it slammed against the wall. "Amy, my love! So glad to see you, darling."

He headed straight to Amy, ignoring Hopkins, but from the side of his eye he saw the man jump. Wheeler walked in front of Amy, blocking her, loudly announcing his departure because he had all his belongings. Filbert was instructing William about something; he wasn't sure what since the blood rushing to his head blocked his hearing. He wrapped his arm around Amy and chattering away, got them both out of the room, Filbert following.

"Out of the house. Now." William dragged Amy outside, holding her in his arms. Filbert was wiping sweat from his brow, looking a tad better than in the drawing room, although still somewhat green.

He heard a gunshot, and within minutes, Hopkins came barreling out the front door, sans gun. William threw himself at the man, both tumbling to the ground. Hopkins shoved him back and jumped up and ran, William after him. He grabbed him by the back of his jacket and swung him around. One good slam into Hopkins' jaw from William's fist and the man went down like a sack of flour.

Wheeler hobbled down the steps, holding his leg, blood dripping onto the pathway.

Hopkins shook his head and started to stand. Amy picked up a decorative rock and slammed him over the head with it. "That is for threatening my child."

They all worked to gain their breath as they stared at the man responsible for two murders passed out on the ground.

"Handcuff him, Wheeler, and then let's all retire to the library for a brandy," William said. He glanced at Filbert. "Summon the doctor." Then he threw his arm around Amy's shoulders and kissed her on the cheek.

She smiled up at him. "Welcome home, Husband."

EPILOGUE

One week later

*A*my yawned and shook her head. "I don't understand why I am so sleepy."

She, William, Aunt Margaret, and Mr. Mackay sat in the drawing room awaiting the announcement for dinner. William and Mr. Mackay held glasses of whisky while Aunt Margaret and Amy had each declined a pre-dinner drink.

She straightened up and looked over at William. "You know, we never did learn who broke into the vicarage and scattered all the files around."

William took a sip of his drink. "I apologize, Wife. I forgot to pass that information along. Mr. Wheeler told me one of the lads from the village did it, looking for money since the vicarage was empty. Mr. Wheeler has the boy washing windows for a few of the businesses in the village as his punishment. I guess the boy assumed there would be money hidden in the files. But then, who knows what a child will think?"

"I'll tell you what I think. I think we did not give enough credit to Mr. Wheeler."

"So it seems."

She yawned again, quite annoyed with herself for this fatigue. "With the house so quiet, it seems that I should be getting a lot of writing done, but I am too sleepy to even do that."

The knocker on the front door followed by a male voice had them looking toward the doorway. Aunt Margaret began to rise from her seat just as Lord Exeter entered the room.

"Jonathan!" She hurried over to him.

He wrapped his arms around her, and she burst into tears.

He leaned back, smiling at her. "I thought you would be glad to see me."

She nodded. "I am," she said as she continued to weep.

William walked up to the man and held his hand out. "Welcome back, Exeter."

Jonathan held Aunt Margaret against his side and took William's hand. "It's good to be back." He reached into his pocket and pulled out a handkerchief that he handed to Aunt Margaret. "Come, my dear, let us sit down."

They walked to the settee that Aunt Margaret had been sitting on and settled in. Amy had never seen her aunt so disconcerted. She hung onto Jonathan's arm with one hand and wiped her cheeks with the other.

"Care for a drink?" William said.

"Yes. A whisky sounds good." He turned Aunt Margaret's head toward him and gave her a rather chaste kiss, but considering they had an audience, that was about all he could do.

He accepted the whisky from William. "I finished much sooner than I thought I would."

Amy stood to find Filbert to tell him there would be another guest for dinner and fought back a bout of dizziness. She looked over at William who regarded her with concern.

When she returned, Mr. Mackay was busy talking to Jonathan as if he'd known him all his life. Mostly he badgered him with questions on his recent trip to Scotland. If Jonathan was confused about exactly who Mr. Mackay was and why he was living with them, he didn't say.

"I assume things have been quiet since I've been gone?"

Everyone in the room except Jonathan laughed. Even Mr. Mackay slapped his thigh and gave quite a chortle.

Jonathan looked from face to face. "What am I missing?"

Aunt Margaret, who seemed to have gained control, patted him on the hand. "I will tell you all about it later."

Amy straightened in her chair, her eyes wide. "Jonathan, how long have you been gone to Scotland?"

He tapped his lips and said, "I believe I left the beginning of September."

"Are you certain it has been that long?"

William looked at her. "What is wrong, my love? You look a tad frightened."

Amy counted on her fingers and sucked in a breath. "William, it appears Charles will have a brother or sister in about seven months!"

While congratulations were being offered, Aunt Margaret hugging Amy and telling her they could raise all their children together, there was another knock on the front door.

After noisy footsteps and voices raised, Eloise walked into the drawing room holding one of the twins—Amy could never tell them apart—followed by Michael holding another twin, followed by Miss Payne, the twins' nanny, followed by two of their footmen carrying several large pieces of luggage.

"Well, sister dear. My wife almost burned down the house trying to cook something for the girls and managed to damage only the kitchen. I'm afraid we will have to stay here for while the repairs are made."

The two little girls began to wail as Filbert announced dinner.

Michael spoke over the noise. "Wethington. A brandy please."

The End

Did you like this story? Please consider leaving a review on either Goodreads or the place where you bought it. Long or short, your review will help other readers discover new authors and make purchasing decisions!

I hope you had fun reading *Death and Deception*. If you'd like to enjoy more mysteries, shop in my online store for big savings!

MYSTERY BOOK BUNDLE
includes
Death and Deception
Homicide at the Vicarage
For the Love of the Baron
The Pursuit of Mrs. Pennyworth
Anyplace But Here

You can find a list of all my books on my website:
http://calliehutton.com/books/

ABOUT THE AUTHOR

USA Today bestselling author, Callie Hutton, author of more than sixty historical romance, romantic suspense, and cozy mystery books, writes humorous and spicy Regency with "historic elements and sensory details" (The Romance Reviews). With a million novels sold and translated into several languages, she continues to entrance readers with her heartfelt historical romances and mysteries. Her Victorian cozy mystery book, *The Sign of Death* was a finalist in the Simon and Schuster Mary Higgins Clark award in 2022. Visit www.calliehutton.com for more information.

Praise for books by Callie Hutton

A Study in Murder

"This book is a delight!...*A Study in Murder* has clear echoes of Jane Austen, Agatha Christie, and of course, Sherlock Holmes. You will love this book." —William Bernhardt, author of *The Last Chance Lawyer*

"A one-of-a-kind new series that's packed with surprises." —Mary Ellen Hughes, National bestselling author of *A Curio Killing*

"[A] lively and entertaining mystery...I predict a long run for this smart series." —Victoria Abbott, award-winning author of The Book Collector Mysteries

"With a breezy style and alluring, low-keyed humor, Hutton crafts a charming mystery with a delightful, irrepressible sleuth." —Madeline Hunter, *New York Times* bestselling author of *Never Deny a Duke*

The Sign of Death

A delightful combination of mystery and romance with some unexpected twists. —*Kirkus Reviews*

"A fun, character-driven mystery."—*Library Journal*

"A clever and entertaining 'whodunnit' novel by an author with an impressive talent and a genuine mastery of the historical mystery genre." —*Midwest Book Review*

"Callie Hutton knows how to keep the reader's attention from the first page until the very last word...The way that Hutton orchestrates things is magical." —*Cozy Mystery Book Reviews*

"Plenty of twists in the plot lines, both mystery and romantic...a pleasant read that lovers of historical cozies should enjoy." — Historical Novel Society

The Mystery of Albert E. Finch

"Cozy fans will have fun." —*Publishers Weekly*

"An extraordinary and unreservedly recommended addition." —*Midwest Book Review*

"There is so very much to love in this book! The wit and humor will keep you smiling even while you are commiserating with poor William who just wants to go on his honeymoon." —Vine Voice

"As like the two previous books, it was fun to follow them on their merry chase as they also try to settle into married life, a bliss everyone seems determined to prevent them to enjoy." — Top 1000 Reviewer, Amazon

Made in the USA
Middletown, DE
02 May 2023